CATHERINE PHIL MACCARTHY has published two collections of poetry, *This Hour of the Tide* (Salmon, 1994) and *The Blue Globe* (Blackstaff Press, 1998). She is a former writer-in-[obscured by sticker]
City of Dublin (1994) and also [obscured by sticker]
One Room an Everywhere is her fir[obscured by sticker]

ONE ROOM AN EVERYWHERE

♦

Catherine Phil MacCarthy

THE
BLACKSTAFF
PRESS

BELFAST

First published in 2003 by
Blackstaff Press Limited
4c Heron Wharf, Sydenham Business Park
Belfast BT3 9LE
with the assistance of
the Arts Council of Northern Ireland

Typeset by Techniset Typesetters, Newton-le-Willows, Merseyside

Printed in Ireland by ColourBooks Limited

A CIP catalogue record for this book is available from the British Library

ISBN 0-85640-741-0

www.blackstaffpress.com

For Justin,
with love

'For love, all love of other sights controules,
And makes one little roome, an every where.'

John Donne, 'The Good-morrow'

ONE

White. Unrelenting. Sunlight pours through the window. I haul the duvet over my head and sink under the covers. A weight nestles at my feet. The half-empty bottle of Black Bush. I have to get up. I pull myself onto my knees and gape in shock. A face I don't recognise in the pocked glass. Eyes swollen and blackened, cheeks stained. I see it's mascara streaked with tears. It'll wash off.

I can't think back yet to the moment whiskey burned my throat and sleep came. A black pool I slipped into without trace. Dreamless. Taken blindfold by some god to another land. My body is still left in this one. I have no mind for it. And now what use are words?

Better to get up, run the bath and watch the steam fog the taps, take some cold cream from the jar, and with a cotton wool pad, begin to clean my face. With a sweep of my arm, I fling the covers back and ease my feet over the side of the bed. My legs take a moment to steady themselves on the worn rug.

2

Hot water plunges from the shiny brass tap into a white cast-iron bath. From the small blue bottle of essential oils, I tip drop after golden drop as the water pours.

Why was it Carol I rang, explaining my need to get away for a few days, to fall through a black space? As if my panic could not be contained by that sunny house, with ivory walls, bookshelves, the small desk, a steel rail of my clothes. The windowpane framed with orange and blue stained glass. It was warm, a safe haven. It smelt of apples and cooking. Fresh flowers. Memories of him. I hankered for isolation. I had to get away from that room where I used to bring him on Saturday afternoons in spring when we were completely alone.

He used to ring in the mornings to ask if I wanted to meet for lunch. Instead of going to a café, I would offer to cook for him. When he arrived, we would eat first. Or not. That initial time, after a self-conscious embrace, he came into the kitchen and we broke apart as if burned. I asked if he knew the road, neighbourhood, this neck of the woods. He held my gaze in a way that made it all right to relax and we sat down to have a drink. When the moment came, we left the laden table for the darkness of the upstairs bedroom.

TWO

'Nothing ever has to happen,' he once said. Then, the first kiss. I was standing at the studio window of his office. I could hear a piano across the narrow passageway and, down below, people on their way home from work. The sky was clear after a dreary winter day, and I breathed the rain-washed air and marvelled at the soft blue among the roofs, the rosy reflection of sun on clouds. It was unusual for me to be there.

Earlier, he had handed me a collection of stories as he turned from his desk. 'Maybe you have the taste for it?'

'Fine,' I said, sounding more relaxed than I felt placing the folder in a leather holdall and anxious at the prospect of influencing a decision. 'I'll let you know what I think in a couple of days.'

I worked as an editor in the publishing house, taking home typescripts to edit and proofs to read. He struck me as friendly and reticent, enunciating his words clearly in a slightly foreign accent. Gradually he passed stories to my desk.

The colour drew me to his dark green eyes that took fright when I looked at him. He'd wait for me to finish speaking, and then he'd relax and I'd become visible again. I was curious about his thoughts during the invisible moments. As if some light between us became a blind spot.

He had lived abroad. This I gathered in previous weeks as I got used to the work and came to understand that he was tireless in his dealings with myself and others; at least fifteen years older, and probably married.

That evening I waited in silence as he watered the geranium seedlings on the windowsill, and the parched earth softened in clay pots. I'd gone regularly to plays and recitals with him, meeting there and saying goodbye afterwards to catch the tube.

Sometimes over coffee or a drink he told stories of places he'd been, and people he'd known. On those occasions it seemed a great gulf separated the past from the present. And now, I wanted to say. What about now? Who do you see and talk to? Who takes your fancy? I never dared. There was a tacit agreement that our current domestic lives were safe from scrutiny.

Patrick was impatient to be clear of the day's work and anxious to be ready.

'All work and no play,' he apologised.

'Why geraniums?' I asked, curious at his watering of plants. Wasn't it something old ladies had time for? Anyway, real gardens, like my mother's, were outdoors.

'They grow wild in the Cape. Big as small trees, with amazing colours.'

'They do?' I gave the tiny leaves a second glance. 'I love that about the world. The way things are different in other places,' I said, as he closed the window.

He glanced at his watch, glad that his work was finished

for the day. His face was pale and smiling.

'I know you prefer jazz,' I said, aware that the Chicago Symphony might be wasted on him, even though Gershwin was on the programme.

'I love going to the Festival Hall,' he assured me.

'You often work late?' I was hoping to elicit details of his personal life.

'When there's no one to distract me,' he said pointedly, closing the small cupboard where he had placed the watering can. 'I like being distracted. Don't you?'

I nodded vaguely. 'Temporarily.'

And now he was beside me, his eyes level with mine. 'Only temporarily?' was his instant reply. 'You're giving me a spoonful of my own medicine, is that it?' The question was so sudden and direct that I didn't know what to say. His eyes rested on my face.

'What's good for the goose?' I answered, noticing the photograph of a young girl on his desk, no more than eight or nine years old.

He followed the direction of my gaze. 'That's my daughter,' he confided, and his right eye flinched in that split-second way it did when he wanted to steer clear of an argument. He reached for the frame and stood closer, the photo in his hands, strong and shapely, dark hair on the back tinged with light. He might be a pianist, I thought, if he could be persuaded to sit still long enough in the one place.

'Hardly my baby any more. It was taken a couple of years ago. Her name is Kate.' He handed me the close-up of a red-haired, freckled girl in swimming togs, her sleek skin beaded with water.

'She's lovely,' I said, gratified by this disclosure of his personal world, but curious about the colour of her hair, the lack of resemblance between them. 'Not like you at all.'

He laughed.

I didn't mean it to sound like he wasn't lovely too. It was hardly the moment to tell him that I liked his rakish brown hair that most days cried out for a comb. Or that I wanted to reach out and rub away the tiny creases that formed at the corner of his eyes when he was tired.

'I've not mentioned her before?' he asked, bringing me back to earth.

'No.' I smiled.

'You might have seen her one Wednesday?' he said. And then added, 'Why are we talking about Kate?'

I placed the photo back on the desk. 'We could pretend she doesn't exist?'

He moved closer, then lifted a strand of hair from beneath the gold chain round my neck.

'Why would we do that?' he asked gently.

'I'm not changing the subject, more raising it,' I ventured, taking in this new knowledge of him as a father. I imagined his home, the girl in the photo, her mother there. 'You like being a parent?'

He hesitated.

'She lives with her mother. I see her mostly at weekends, holiday time. You know . . . '

No, I thought, I don't know. How do you manage to be so . . . ? Inscrutable.

He observed my reaction.

His eyes guardedly met mine. 'Nothing ever has to happen.' He spoke softly.

'Something always does,' I whispered then, holding his gaze.

The contact of his thumb pressing on my collarbone was live as the current of an electric fence I brushed once, crossing a field. I stood by the window, overwhelmed by the physical proximity of his body, unable to say anything. Neither of us moved.

From the passageway below, the sound of a door banged

and voices clamoured as people left the office and made their way to the street. The building was deserted.

What he said next I hardly heard. When his lips touched mine for the first time they were warm and deliberate, the way a current in the sea is warm, bathing my whole body as it lifts against the swell.

THREE

The sensation of the kiss stayed with me like a spell for days afterwards. And the knowledge that there was something untrammelled in Patrick's nature. I thought of my father. The day he fought with my mother. He called her a bitch. He had a brush in his hand. They were standing in the kitchen. The force of his voice struck my ears. The way a big wave might, as it slapped over my shoulder, its force knocking me down and tumbling me in its wake.

'You can walk out now, but if you do, you won't come back,' my mother said. What caused her to speak in that way? No, I thought, please don't go. Can you not see how upset she is? She doesn't mean it. I wanted to say it out loud, but he was already taking his coat from the hanger in the hall. Suddenly he looked very tall, my father, and very white, as he walked through the front door in his greatcoat, his back turned towards me.

He would go to the Hanleys', I decided. Ellen was seven

years older than me, seventeen that summer. She looked after us when my parents went to town for the afternoon, and joined in when we knelt on the sand, sea water dripping from our swimsuits, to scoop a moat round a castle we were making, her long, dark ponytail falling over her shoulder. Would my father walk across the strand or around by the road? If the tide was low, it would only take half an hour. But already on the way in, it would be safer by road. The Hanleys would take him in until the storm blew over.

What if I had to choose one or the other? If I stayed, did it mean I was siding with my mother? And what about my small brother? Would Connor and I have to chose one or the other and then part forever?

Connor was playing at the back of the house with an old trailer. He hauled it time and again to the top of the grassy bank beneath the fuchsia hedge that ran all round the garden. The bank was higher at the back of the house and sloped gently to the yard. Once on top, he sat himself inside it, gripped the reins attached to the front and slid down as fast as possible. The little trailer ran across the paved yard. I could hear the wheels coursing cement as my father's feet crunched on gravel. He walked briskly to the gate, past the hedge that had no blossoms yet, and down the lane, a solitary figure in his dark coat, white clouds boiling into the blue. I watched him disappear.

Some time later my father's clothes, dark suits and coats, which used to hang in the big wardrobe in their bedroom, lay in a deep pile on the spare bed in the room where Connor slept. I used to run my hand in the folds along the silky lining of his jacket sleeves and read the writing on the labels on the inside pocket. I asked my mother if he was moving into Connor's room. She said nothing. I looked closely at her then, waiting for an answer, but she turned away. First it was his clothes, then his work things. Finally himself. The house felt empty and quiet for days.

Occasionally the phone rang, with people looking for him for building work. They were given another number. Gradually the calls stopped. He rarely rang to speak to my mother. She hardly encouraged it.

I recalled again the sinking feeling I'd had all those years ago, as the car was loaded up with his things. When it was all done, he lifted Connor and myself one by one in his arms. Bonnie jumped up and down and barked. Dad promised to come back often. I watched the tyres rumbling over fresh gravel, and imagined being run over by the car.

FOUR

From the start, seeing Patrick felt out of bounds. Sometimes we ran into each other on the stairs, or he phoned with questions on the content of a particular script. I left the office in the evenings, walking to the train with a feeling of relief in my new-found life. This job was very different from the academic research I'd previously done. Beneath the relief came disquiet. I wondered about the city, the air it gave of everything being possible. London was mostly unknown to me.

A new silence enfolded us both when we met. Over coffee in the office with the others, the tone of his voice seemed to address me in particular, and his eyes lightened and softened as he looked across at me from the easy chair. I tried to appear at ease when he handed me a cup and saucer, sitting alongside Carol, with whom I shared an office and who helped me deal calmly and swiftly with the volumes of copy that landed on my desk.

As I made my way home on the train I imagined his tongue finding mine, as it did at the end of the concert. He had sat through the music like a listless horse. I turned to him as we got to our feet and he drew me against him until my feet lifted from the floor.

It reminded me of how limp my body grew and how light my head became on those nights I sat at the top of the stairs kissing Denis, outside the door of the flat in Dublin I shared with a friend. The dark in the long window at the return began to grow blue. Sometimes a first bird started up before he left. Going down the stairs he would take an apple from the pocket of his cord jacket and place it in my hand, before he drew a cap from the other and walked down the stairs whistling. A neat reversal of Adam and Eve. If the story of original sin included all about kisses, then it might have been easier to understand, I decided, as the train came to a halt near the station where I lived.

Walking home under the bare beeches of the park, I noticed the rich green daffodil shoots under the trees. Old life giving way to the new. Is that how it always is? The lighted Georgian windows revealed sitting rooms with fires already lit, worlds inside a play. In one, people were seated around a dining table. Terracotta pink walls, hung with prints and paintings, framed the convivial gathering round a table covered in white linen. It all looked close enough to touch. I wondered how people could sip from their glasses and be so freely open to inspection. As I walked along the railings, basement kitchens peeped back at me. If I could enter one of them, and sit down at a table, what secrets would they disclose? There were young children playing at the corner of the square. My step quickened as I reached the street where I lived and the house that was home.

I turned the key in the door and from the hall saw that Sam was already home and preparing the dinner, the evening news spilling from the radio. As I climbed the stairs, I called hello, and he called back, letting me know that there was cold wine in the fridge and that Sue would be home by seven. My room was almost dark. I lay on the bed listening to sounds from the kitchen.

As my limbs sank into the quilt I thought about Denis. Of how he pleaded with me not to leave. Our lives had become sheeted from each other, the way the surface of the sea in Dublin Bay is often sheeted, pearly white and insubstantial. And so still. An ebbing tide. We walked the shoreline sometimes in the late afternoon on Sundays and caught glimpses of a car ferry turning on the horizon as it made for harbour, or a lone heron standing still in the shallows in the filling tide. Sometimes a horse galloped by, urged on by its rider, the sound of the hoofs ringing in the air. Often those walks ended in arguments. Usually the same one. I was restless and, once my research contract ended in the summer, ready to move. Denis was happy with things as they were, finding his way in his first job as site engineer.

It was difficult to name the impulse propelling me forward into another world that started with knowing him. When his older sister Sue had completed her medical training in Dublin, she went to work at a health centre in London as a children's doctor, where she met Sam. I had travelled across with Denis to stay with them for a long weekend and then for their wedding, which was probably when the idea of living in London began to take hold.

In the end I started to apply for jobs in publishing there and travelled across for an interview. The company was willing to see the first six months as a training period and offered me the job. Even though Denis didn't quite believe I would go, he wrote to Sue of my plans, and she rang offering to rent me a room.

After four months, this new life was more real and familiar than the old one. I grew used to the patterns in the house, to the mixture of company and solitude, and to weekends when Sam and Sue went to stay with friends in Devon or at his parents' home on the Essex coast and the place was entirely my own.

The week before, Adele had invited me to consider working on a new project: stories aimed at the teenage market. Next day, when I popped in to her office to let her know that I would take on the editing of the new series, she was working with Patrick. I opened the door and saw him and wanted to close it again. The small briefcase I carried in one hand found itself folded inside my crossed arms. Adele looked over her glasses from the text she was reading.

'We're working on next year's catalogue,' she explained. 'We've just finished the list but I haven't tackled today's post yet. We might speak after that?' She indicated a tray of correspondence.

I looked at Patrick, who was noting something on a script.

'I'd like to take on the new project.'

'The teenage series,' Adele said to Patrick. 'We discussed it last month and you came up with the idea? Since then I've put it to Eve.'

He gave me a cursory glance. His face was impassive. Was this the man I'd kissed? Perhaps he had thought better of it?

Adele turned to me. 'I'm really glad. You can always use me as a sounding board. I wouldn't mind running it myself.'

'I've got to face Grace Mason later. Any chance you wouldn't mind running that?' Patrick asked her as he stood up. He stretched his arms behind his head lazily and yawned.

'She's all yours,' Adele laughed. 'Maybe Eve can come to the rescue?'

I walked to the door.

Patrick picked up his keys. 'This author likes to talk. I'll never get out of there,' he protested to Adele as he left the room. 'Have you not met her?' he said to me as he closed the door behind us.

'Not yet,' I said hopefully.

'What about a coffee?'

I glanced at my watch. It was just after nine. The invitation was a surprise. Patrick obviously started work much earlier.

We went down the back stairs, down three flights and out the side door to where the aroma of fresh coffee wafted in the blustery air by the café.

Once inside, he turned to me. 'You've got something in your eye.' He looked intently at my face.

I could feel nothing but rubbed both eyes anyway.

'Let's see.' He brushed my eyelid gently. 'There,' he said, satisfied, extracting a speck of sleep on his nail.

'The house white?' The woman's face was dun with freckles under wavy auburn hair as she gave him the eye.

'Two, Maisie. Please. That was some storm last night?'

'Kate's put a stop to his gallop,' she said, turning to me with a wink. 'Now that she's growing up he has even less time on his hands.' Her brown eyes rested speculatively on my face.

I threw a vague quizzical look at Patrick.

'Is that so, Maisie!' He was unperturbed as he fished for his wallet in the pocket of his jacket and extracted a note.

Maisie's lips closed in a pout as she turned her back to steam the milk and then filled the cup to the brim with Italian coffee.

Patrick placed the note on the counter and handed me a cup.

'Haven't seen your face before. Are you a young author?' she asked, placing the change on the counter.

'Good God, no!' I laughed as she turned to the open copy of the *Daily Mail*.

Relieved to be left alone, we settled into the high swivel seats by the window. He was relaxed and his elbow touched mine slightly. Beyond the window, the wind was carrying a pink balloon along the path. It was sprinkled with glitter and trailed a silver ribbon. It looked lost, buffeted by the wind, on the grey pavement, like a child's dream whipped from the hand.

He stirred his coffee meditatively. 'Italian's my favourite, strong and black when the chips are down.'

'When are the chips down?' I asked, thinking of how I used to find my mother sitting at the kitchen table with her head in her hands that winter my father left.

'When the printers are screaming for copy and the author is having a brain wave and wants to change the ending.' He spooned the cream from his cup into his mouth.

Patrick's answer was so rooted in practical day-to-day chaos that we both laughed and we talked about work for a while.

'Long time no see,' he said later, quietly looking at me.

I felt the heckling winter sun on my face through the window, along with his eyes. It was starting to rain.

'It may be February on the street, but it's August in here,' he continued, rubbing his chest.

I smiled.

'What are you thinking?' he asked.

'That new project Adele suggested. You came up with the idea for teenage books?'

'I'm familiar with the age group. I didn't mean work just now.' He paused. 'Kate's coming to stay at the weekend. She wants to go to the pictures. Likes oldies and there's a Bogart season in our local cinema.' He looked at me keenly. 'Would you like to join us? Would you enjoy that?'

Patrick liked films too. He was so interested in books I didn't think there would be any time left for cinema. He raised his eyebrows, waiting for my response. 'I'd like you to meet Kate,' he said encouragingly and drained the last of his coffee.

Maisie was chatting to another customer. I moved to the door and he followed. Drops of rain blew in the wind. We ran together to the side door and went inside, me to climb the stairs and Patrick to speak to Tony, the designer, whose office was on the ground floor.

'I'll call you later,' I said airily.

'Come to my office at five and ask if I'm coming to the meeting. I'll come straight out.' I could see that he was at a loss for words, standing there with his hands by his sides.

I went upstairs to my office. My heart was beating, only partly from running up the stairs. I was glad to be alone. I hung the short wool jacket I was wearing on the back of the chair. New shoes pinched my heels. The skylight window sung with the beat of rain and the patter gradually calmed the rise and fall of my breathing. Why did Patrick want me to meet Kate? Wouldn't she rather have her father to herself?

When I knocked on the door at a quarter to five, there was no answer. I was about to turn away when I heard a woman's voice. I knocked again. He finally called, 'Come in.'

Two women in flowing robes were sitting opposite Patrick. After Botticelli. Mother and daughter, I concluded instantly. Patrick looked anything but unhappy, his legs stretched forward, hands behind his head, listening to the person I decided was the mother. Neither turned her head to look at me and I noticed how smooth and fair the daughter's complexion was, and how beautiful she was. Behind Patrick's desk, the window opened onto a view of rooftops. The older woman was relating the story of a party she'd hosted the week before.

Patrick looked across at me. 'Eve!' He jumped to his feet, glancing at his watch, and waved me to come in. 'Is it that time already? I'm dreadfully sorry. Do forgive me, Grace, and meet Eve Bennett, our youngest recruit from across the water.'

Both women stood now, blond hair falling over their shoulders. The younger turned her pale green smiling eyes on me and I extended a hand.

'Deirdre Mason,' she said gently. Her mulberry dress of crushed velvet fell all the way to the top of her Doc Martens.

I scanned her mother's plump and weathered face for similarities, as the older woman extended a cursory hand.

'Irish?' she asked.

I nodded.

'From where?' she commanded.

I mentioned the local town.

'Wonderful place. I'm fond of the Irish,' she commented. 'Never short of a good yarn' – and to Patrick – 'it's so improved these days, don't you think?' Without waiting for an answer, she went on to describe how very frugal it was 'some years ago now, when we went there first but very charming even then.' She turned to me again. 'You have a lovely country, dear,' she assured me.

I smiled at her doubtfully.

'We must go. Come Deirdre, the Pennyfeathers are expecting us for supper.' With that she picked up the folder that lay on the desk, and the two women swept from the room, leaving a faint air of musk scent behind them.

Patrick noted something in his diary and gathered loose pages into a file. 'Come, I'll walk you to the train,' he said.

Nobody left the office before five thirty and it was often six or later when deadlines were tight.

'Now?' I said, looking at my watch.

He was already on his feet and taking his coat from the hook at the back of the door.

'Even better, we could walk over Primrose Hill, and you could take the Northern line?'

'Great.' I had to agree it would be easier to talk outside the office.

Along the street the tarmac was slippy, and the February trees were black against the sky. Streetlights were already coming on. The collar of his woollen overcoat was pulled close by a grey scarf. We walked through the park gate and fell into step as we followed the path to the crest of the hill.

'If Saturday doesn't suit . . . ' he began, and when I did not reply, 'Kate will want to go anyway. We might catch an early show.'

We walked on in silence. Cold air seeped round us as we stopped to look down at the city below, lying in a misty light.

'There's St Paul's and the river.' He indicated a distant point on the horizon. I could see several spires. 'And Big Ben.'

I looked at the tapestry of lights, the mesh of skyscrapers that stood against the darkening horizon.

We stopped again next to a hawthorn, whose branches offered a filigree shade.

'The cinema's about twenty minutes from where you live. What about three thirty on Saturday?' he said.

I could have said no, but his eyes were so green and shining and he was looking at me with such calm expectation that I thought, what harm? What harm could there be in going to a matinee with him and his daughter?

'If Kate doesn't mind . . . ' I relented.

'Kate's often met the others at work. Why should I keep you a secret?' he said casually.

He had known them for years. It told me how easily his personal life meshed with the office. He would pass me off as a colleague. It was more or less true.

'Because . . . ' I began to say, but stopped.

'Because?' he mused, reaching for my cold hand.

My coat fell open. I was unable to close it again because of the briefcase weighing my free arm. He looked suddenly boyish, despite his years, damp hair glistening in the fading light.

'Because I haven't done this with Adele or Carol?' He stopped and laid a hand on the top button of my shirt and looked at me directly.

'Something like that,' I muttered. My body was tense. I like my job, I wanted to say.

He smiled then and shrugged and we continued walking.

'London's a big place,' he said emphatically.

'You're still my boss.'

'Adele is,' he said, taken aback.

We were approaching the bottom of the hill. His pace quickened.

'You in a rush?' I called out.

He turned and waited with his hands deep in the pockets of his overcoat.

'Where are we headed?'

'You tell me,' he said quietly, as I caught up with him.

In silence, we moved closer for a kiss. His hand was under my coat and round my waist. The other again found the top button of my shirt and opened it, moving to the second with deliberate ease. My breathing quickened.

A shiver in the branches behind us shook drops from the tree. He hesitated as youths strolled towards us on their way down the hill, their jibes and laughter at each other, lewd and raucous. They were young men, closer in age to me than he was. My body grew tense as we waited for them to pass.

'Let me hold you,' he said evenly. 'They'll be gone in a second.'

I rested in his arms and we began to kiss lightly, ignoring the voices that gradually became distant, as Patrick nibbled my lower lip. Then, one by one, he did up the buttons of my coat, as deliberately as he had unbuttoned my blouse, and ended by folding the scarf around my ears.

We walked through the gate together and crossed the road to the dark entrance of the station. On the platform Patrick waited with me for the train.

'If Kate knows from the beginning too . . . ' It was cold on the platform and I blew on my fingers to keep them warm.

'Kate?' I fingered the material.

'She's been to Ireland. She liked Dingle,' he said encouragingly. 'You'll see.'

'You actually stayed in the town?' It was my home town and he had already been there.

'A mile or two on the western side.' He mentioned the townland and family name of the hotel where they spent several days, a couple of miles from where I grew up. He knew I'd been home for Christmas, for five short days.

'I hardly notice when I'm at home, but every time I leave I miss the salt air and the light.' I sighed.

'I'm not surprised.' He smiled.

'I even miss things that used to drive me mad when I was at home.'

'Like what?'

'The stink of fish on the pier. My mother's concern. The way Denis lit a cigarette for me from his own and placed it between my lips.'

'Who's Denis?'

'My ex-boyfriend. We got to know each other at college in Dublin. He used to take me for rides on the boat. He's from Dingle too. He knew my father. Don't you miss Cape Town?' I said, avoiding this focus on me.

'What would I miss?' he said impatiently, adding that he no longer took an interest in news from South Africa.

His response puzzled me. 'Do you ever feel homesick?'

'My home is in here.' He placed a hand on his heart. 'I carry it with me.'

Very convenient, I thought, but didn't say. It beats being torn apart.

Down the track, the signal light changed from red to green. The platform was already crowded.

'You miss the sunshine?'

'I miss the clouds. Not just any old clouds. I used to watch them from our back yard pour over Table Mountain into a blue sky. They were white and dynamic, like plumes of smoke from a fire pouring down on the city like a god's anger.' He had grown pale and his voice moved back in his throat as he spoke. 'You'll have to see.'

'One day, maybe.' I glanced at him quickly. 'What about your family? It's a lot to give up.'

'Lots of people left in those days.' He tried to sound casual and rubbed his hands together to keep warm.

'Have you gone back since the elections?' I asked.

'Not since my father died in ninety-one. My mother likes to come to London at Christmas.'

'Don't you want to see the changes?'

His detachment was beginning to feel immoral. 'I never wanted to be a tourist in my own country.'

'Going home for Christmas makes me a tourist?' I was stung. We could hear the noise of a train.

'Of course not.'

'What then?'

One light along the track slowly became two as the train drew near.

'I was seventeen when I left and I'm forty-four now. You might decide not to stay.'

I said nothing for a moment. I was twenty-six and too busy counting the gap in years. The train came to a halt and the doors were opening. I drew his scarf from round my neck, but he restrained my hand.

'Keep it. You have a ten-minute walk from the train. Bring it on Saturday.'

'Thanks,' I said. 'Even if I stay, I'll never stop going there, it'll always be a part of me.'

I moved towards a door and waited as the last passengers got off. He stayed close beside me.

'It'll be a part of you, whether you go or not.'

I stepped on to the carriage.

'Now you know my age,' he said. He waited on the

platform. 'Phone me tomorrow with your address.'

The doors closed between us. He waved as the train moved off.

When I got home an hour later I resisted the impulse to take off my blouse and lay in the dusk, absorbing the memory of his hands.

FIVE

The car that drew up three days later was an old black Citroën DS Pallas, the kind I'd often seen in films. In panic I had tried on almost everything in my limited wardrobe and the bed was strewn with underwear, tights and skirts. There was no time to tidy them away when the doorbell rang.

I opened it to find a young girl, arm in arm with her father.

'Phew! Dad's friends are usually older than you.' She looked from him to me.

He smiled and asked if I was ready to go. I picked up a jacket from the hanger in the hall, along with a leather backpack.

Once we reached the car, Patrick held the back door open for Kate.

'Do I have to?' she said, and when he firmly nodded she turned to me. 'If you weren't here, I'd be able to sit in the front.'

Patrick and I exchanged a glance.

'Come on, Kate,' he said in exasperation. 'Get in the car.'

I was reminded of my brother, who was well able to argue over which car seat we sat in, but not in front of total strangers.

'Let's toss for it,' I suggested. 'Head or harp?' I drew a coin from my wallet.

'Harp?' she said mockingly. 'You mean tails. Heads, of course.'

I flicked the coin and it rolled onto the pavement. Kate stamped on it.

'Let's see,' Patrick said.

She lifted her suede boot and bent to pick up the coin. 'You win,' she said sulkily. 'But I sit in the front on the way home.'

Patrick raised his eyebrows and threw me another glance.

'It starts at four,' he said impatiently to Kate. 'Come on, let's go.'

I slipped into the front passenger seat. Soft leather squeaked. Patrick switched on the ignition and the car began to rise like a hovercraft. Kate sprawled across the back seat, her head resting on her hand.

'Are you from Ireland?' she asked suddenly.

'Yes,' I replied.

'From where, then?' She looked with new interest.

'Eve's from Dingle,' her father intervened. 'Remember where we went to stay on the farm, and you made friends with a boy in Ventry?'

Kate sat up on the seat.

'No, I didn't. John Lynch wasn't my friend. He was Laura's,' she countered. Then she suppressed a smile. 'He loved stunts. They used to come on their bikes. The road from the gate to the house was really fast and they put ramps along it and timed everyone. John Lynch usually won. He didn't care how fast he went, even if he killed himself.'

Patrick sped along, turning left when he got to Highgate and taking short cuts where he could find them. The luxury of seeing London over-ground was not lost on me. The redbrick terraces grew larger and the spaces more generous, the closer we came to Hampstead.

'You liked him?' I asked Kate, who was gathering her long red mane into a hairband.

'He was all right,' she replied. 'He had a ponytail. I reckon Laura O'Neill fancied him. On our last night he asked me to a disco after the carnival. Dad was livid with me the following day.' She looked at her father, who was parking the car on a quiet laneway.

'We don't need to go over that again, Kate.' He turned to me. 'The cinema's just round the corner.'

'I wore my shortest miniskirt,' Kate said, 'and Dad was really furious. It's not my fault he doesn't like miniskirts. He was born in the Ark,' she added defiantly.

I concealed a smile and tried to avoid Patrick's eyes.

'It wasn't just the skirt,' Patrick explained. 'Young Lynch had borrowed a motorbike from his elder brother. He was only fourteen and Kate was twelve last summer.'

She sunk her hands in the pocket of her padded jacket, as we walked down the street together.

'It was dead cool,' she confided to me, then caught her father's sleeve. 'Can we go back next summer?'

We arrived at the cinema and joined the queue for tickets.

'I'd like a Coke and popcorn,' Kate said, eyeing the counter, already three deep with customers. 'I need to pee,' she added and went off to the ladies', stealing a veiled look at me as she left.

Patrick bought the tickets and ordered Coke and popcorn

from the bar. I glanced at him in amusement.

'If you really want to inflame me, now you know what to do,' he suggested.

People filed past us into the cinema.

'Wear my shortest miniskirt and find a boyfriend with a motorbike?' I teased.

'Sorry about the drama,' he said quickly. 'Kate likes to make her presence felt. Don't take it personally.'

She walked towards us, and we retreated to the darkness of the auditorium.

We took our seats just as the house lights went down.

'Prepare to be bored silly,' Kate whispered to me confidentially. 'It's something called *The African Queen*.'

I listened in surprise. Why that film to taunt and beckon? 'I've seen it, a few summers ago,' I whispered back, but Kate was already gazing at the screen.

When the film ended she was immediately on her feet, and we followed her to the exit.

'All that perfectly good gin. Wasn't she wonderful?' The teenager gritted her teeth in a Hepburn smile as we walked down the steps. 'He was just a pushover if you ask me,' she said to her father.

'He'd been alone for a long time on the river. He was used to African ways, unsure how to treat people, especially women.'

Kate glanced from her father to me and said nothing. We were on the street now, milling with late shoppers and traffic.

'When you were in Africa did you ever go down a river like that?' she asked.

Patrick shook his head. 'We lived in a city. I was your age, went to an English school.' He turned to me. 'Wouldn't mind going back, actually.'

'To see those clouds on Table Mountain,' I reminded him.

Kate looked at us. 'They never gave up on each other.

That's what I liked. Even when there was no hope, he didn't walk off and leave her.' Her voice rose in anger and accusation.

'For God's sake, Kate, don't throw that at me.'

Patrick was angry and I walked ahead out of earshot. The remark brought my father to mind, the day I glimpsed him in town with Ellen Hanley, years after he left my mother. Her black hair fell loose to her shoulders, and they were both wearing green rain macks and wellies and they strolled at a leisurely pace, a child with golden curls hand-in-hand between them. Ellen was talking and my father was smiling, and I wanted to call out to him but they were on the far side of the street and didn't see me. The sight of the child stung deeply. I wondered what my mother would say. My cheeks burned and I stood hidden in the doorway of a wool shop. I examined the patterns of the Aran sweaters. Diamond, cable, blackberry, my fingers traced stitches that were once so individual to a family they helped identify fishermen lost at sea.

Behind me I heard Patrick's voice insisting, 'I work with Adele and Carol, as I do with Eve.'

I sighed.

Kate muttered something that I couldn't hear and they walked the rest of the way to the car in silence.

'I'll take you home,' Patrick apologised to me. 'Kate, we'll take Eve back and then I'll make us something to eat.'

He unlocked the car.

She turned to me. 'Has he shagged you yet?' she murmured, slipping into the front, loud enough for her father to hear.

As I took the back seat, she looked at me insistently, chewing a tab of gum she'd found in her pocket and blowing bubbles.

Patrick was furious, I could tell, but only said, 'Eve, Kate's had a difficult week. She and I need to talk. I apologise on her behalf.' His eyes met mine in the rear-view mirror.

Kate switched on the radio. Her eyes were closed and she hummed along with the voice of Lene Marlin. 'I'm sitting down here now, but hey you can't see me, kinda invisible, you don't sense my stay ...' Her lovely insolent face was rapt as she listened to the music. She put her feet on the dashboard and turned up the volume.

Patrick looked again at me, a stoical expression on his face, and drove in silence. His hand rested on the gearstick. The car glided smoothly downhill like a boat in water. When we came to a stop outside my house, I turned to say goodbye to Kate. She was wearing sunglasses she found in the glove compartment and she gave me a cheesy smile.

'See ya!' she said.

Patrick followed me to the doorway and into the hall. His hands fell awkwardly by his sides.

'I'm sorry,' he said. 'You got the rough end of the stick.'

'It's nothing to do with me. I enjoyed the film.' I was annoyed that Patrick had exposed me to Kate's anger.

'She's never forgiven me for leaving Gilly,' he said resignedly.

'It wasn't such a good idea then?' I suggested, leaning against the wall behind me. The large hallway felt suddenly smaller, and as the light shone it cast a warm glow and there was something disarming in Patrick's lean and troubled face.

'She's never seen me with a date.' He appealed. 'There has to be a first.'

'I was the first?' The prospect of becoming a learning curve for Kate was not on my agenda. 'What did you say about me?'

'What is there to say?' he asked, gesturing with his open hands. 'You joined the office a few months ago. We work together. We hardly know each other but I'd like to know you better.' He paused. 'I fall asleep thinking about making love with you.' His voice was coming from somewhere deep and still and one hand reached across the space between us to lightly brush my elbow.

'You said that?' My cheeks were going red.

'Course not. Only that we work together and you don't know London yet.' He lifted his hands to the back of his head and stretched, shrugging off all concern like a cat shrugging off sleep.

'We don't just work together,' I corrected him.

'Kate's already gathered that,' he said with a deep sigh.

Touching felt out of bounds and my feet were rooted to the floor.

'I'd better go. What about lunch during the week? We could start again.' He smiled.

'Kate's probably asleep with boredom by now.' I looked in the direction of the street.

He slipped his hands into the hip pockets of his cords. He was reluctant to leave. 'See you on Monday?'

'We'll talk then. See ya,' I said. He turned to the door and was quickly gone.

SIX

My father was a loner, like Charlie in *The African Queen*. It played in New York at a small cinema across the road from Circle in the Square in the Village, one summer when I was working on a student visa. I sat in the dark afterwards, not wanting to leave. The scene where the boat was landlocked, only for them to realise by morning they were free, made me breathe deeply. It reminded me of my mother's implacable will and my father's truculence. Had they ever found the kind of harmony the film revealed?

When I returned home at the end of that summer, I finally asked my mother why Dad had left for good. I imagined it had to do with some deep lack, the way my father described sites that yielded nothing but trouble when he was sinking a well, only broken machinery and no water when he hit rock. So he had taken to wandering and she had become irascible and broody.

'I assumed you knew why your father and myself . . . ' She left the sentence unfinished.

'That time you fought and told him not to come back?'

She flinched. 'You have a very selective memory.'

I ignored the carp.

She was sitting at a teak table in the kitchen, sanded to the grain and lovingly restored. I'd made a cold soup of tomatoes, cucumber and onion I learnt about from a flatmate, and placed two bowls on the table. Sunlight streaked in the window onto my bare shoulders and motes hung in the air as we tasted it.

'There were very good times. You were the apple of his eye.'

'So much for that.'

'He used to sing "She Moved Through the Fair" and "Raglan Road" when you were a baby. He would have his arms around me and I would have my arms around you. Don't you remember how he sang to us?'

I was silent.

'It was unbearable for a couple of years. Connor was only five the year your father took up with Ellen. She had gone back to school again to study for her exams at the Institute in Dublin. Chemistry was always her best subject and even though her chances of doing medicine were out by then, with a good Leaving Cert she could qualify and teach afterwards or take up a job in a laboratory or a hospital. Your father had subcontracted work in Dublin that year and sometimes he gave her a lift when she was going back after the weekend. I suppose she was very lonely. The day you saw us fight I had to get used to the idea that it was no longer us that mattered. Someone else took all his care. That was the hardest part.'

My mother got up to go in search of an album and returned to the table with a photo of herself and my father, taken in the early days before they married. To my eyes they were young, almost my own age, and handsome in a Buddy Holly way.

'You were always cross with him.' I wanted to know the truth.

'There was you and Connor to look after as well as my teaching job. We had our hands full.' Her back was to the light. She pulled a wrap close. Outside swifts dipped and called and flew past the gable end of the house.

'So why did he leave?' I asked.

'Why did you never ask your father that?' she said, looking again at the photo of him in her hand.

Ellen and my father when she was only twenty? Where did they go? What had they done? She had taught us to play cards and to sing the words of songs that ran in her head. We had sat upstairs at the dressing-table mirror in my bedroom and she'd made up my face with her own make-up. She would do up my hair in a roll at the back of my head and paint my face, finishing with mascara and lipstick and different colour shadings around my eyes. It never occurred to me that she had anything to do with my parents' separation until my mother spoke about it years later.

She broke the silence. 'Once he started with Ellen . . . of course, she was much younger, more compliant than I was. She eventually continued her studies in science and took a job at one of the hospitals. They were involved for years.' She sighed and I could see her face relax, and she put the photo back in its page in the album.

'We managed,' I said gently, regretting my previous outburst. 'Didn't we?'

'More than that.' She laughed then, and we got up to clear away the table.

So that was why my father settled in Dublin. Why had he not told me? And it was why I wanted to live there too while I was in college, as if by living there I might have raised the dead and come to understand him better.

SEVEN

Gilly had chosen him. That much I knew. They met through friends. He was involved in a CND demonstration in London. A sit-down protest in front of Downing Street. When the police arrived with batons and fierce dogs, nobody moved. Patrick was hauled off to the station and tried to punch a policeman. They responded by knocking him to the ground and handcuffing him.

'Do your parents realise where you are?' they shouted. He was twenty-two.

'My parents are out there organising it.' He laughed as he told me about it. 'It was worth it just to see their faces. I was only trying it on. My mother was a member of the ANC and involved in anti-apartheid demonstrations in Cape Town, and if we'd lived here, she would have supported CND.' We were talking over a drink a few evenings after the fiasco with Kate.

Of course it left the police in no doubt as to what to do

with him. He was kicked a few times in the ribs and thrown in a cell. It was Gilly who reported him missing when he didn't arrive home that night, and Gilly who turned up at the police station next morning. As a law student, she promised to take responsibility for him, and explained that he came from a good home and hadn't been in trouble before. The older officer on duty appreciated her concern. Finally, Patrick asked to have a word in confidence. The arrest had taught him a lesson, he said. He would not offend again. Asked for his release as a favour to the young woman, who was his girlfriend. The policeman gave in, but warned that no such leniency could be expected a second time round. Gilly took his hand. They started dating that week.

That sense of injustice and potent rebelliousness struck a cord with me. A very Irish trait.

'A quarter Welsh,' Patrick said then.

That he'd already been married and fathered a child made me envious of his past. I imagined the three of them together in an intimate cocoon.

The setting sun was shining on the stained glass of the bar window, so that we were talking in a rosy pool of light, and I sat still as he leaned back on the leather upholstery of the seat and recounted the story.

He used to meet her after work for a drink, as he did with me, not knowing whether they were going to walk home together afterwards to her place or his. He knew the delicious surprise of making love with her for the first time. And he savoured the random possibilities that each encounter threw up, of meeting or touching and uncovering, the pleasure of discovering someone in all their moods before waking up together every day.

It seemed unfair that their relationship began to come apart precisely because they were willing to forfeit the randomness and uncertainty for a lifetime of waking up side by side each day and having a child together. Is this why Kate wages war on Patrick? I wondered. Somewhere inside she had locked the memory of those early years and was still fighting to sustain them.

When he got to the part where Gilly was pregnant again, his speech slowed as if the act of remembering was an effort.

'Do I have to go on with this?' he said finally, moving the whiskey he'd ordered around in his glass as if the taste of it was slightly sickening. He had already loosened his tie and opened the top button of his shirt. His shoulders were hunched, as he sat looking into his glass.

'Kate gave me the impression that it's not over, that's all,' I persisted.

He went on to tell me how thrilled they were at the prospect of another child, a playmate for Kate and all that. Gilly lost that baby and two more after it. Then she threw herself into her work. It was survival at the time, but it meant that she was hard to reach.

'It seemed to taint who we were, or to challenge our images of each other. She had been the capable one, always in control. The failed pregnancies made Kate more treasured in my eyes. She was just learning to walk and talk . . .' He pushed the glass of whiskey away. It slid across the polished mahogany table and stopped short of crashing to the floor.

We were sitting side by side and our shoulders touched.

'What would Kate say now?' I asked.

'Maybe you should ask her,' he said sharply.

His eyes were dark and his face pale. I wanted to hold him then, to lay him down next to me outside on the grass in the sunshine. To taste the whiskey on his breath and feel his body against mine until it was free of loss. But it was almost March and in the mornings when I crossed Highbury Fields, crystals of ice lay in the grass like diamond bracelets vanishing into the ground under the sun's rays.

'You're a good listener,' he said, as if it had just dawned on him. 'Haven't you had enough?'

'Is there more?' I asked.

Gilly had continued to work hard at the bar, and took silk after several years. He drifted into other relationships and when she got wind of it, she asked him to leave.

'So you left.'

'Kate wanted me to stay. She was going on seven and really beginning to speak up for herself. Then she wanted to come with me but Gilly wouldn't hear of it. On Wednesdays I collect her from school and I have her every other weekend. I would have done anything to keep her, so I gave up the girlfriends and made new friends like Carol. It was better all round.' He smiled. 'Now you have it all,' he said, affecting an Irish brogue.

'So I do.' I smiled back at him.

'Kate's holding out an olive branch. Asked if you'd like to join us tomorrow?' he said suddenly, looking at me tentatively as if what he had already told me was a kind of test, and I would from now on think better of seeing him.

I wanted to say no, and I wanted to say yes.

'I'm not sure it's the right thing. Kate has probably good reason to be angry.' That she had asked was a positive sign, and I decided that the chances of her goodwill holding would increase if I refused. Anyway, I wanted to see him alone.

'Come on,' he said quietly. 'It's the zoo for God's sake. A family outing.'

'I'm not family.'

'She's got a school project. We're only going for an hour.'

'I've got work to do.'

Normally I didn't take time off in the middle of the working week.

'It's a one-off, her idea. Please?' He coaxed.

I wasn't convinced.

'What do you say?' he asked again, and this time I gave in.

*

Kate stood behind us in the reptile house, looking over her father's shoulder at the python.

'The animal I hate most in the world,' she said fervently as we peered through the glass at the speckled dun skin coiled in apparent slumber. She moved away to the tortoises, barely looking at the snake as if the very sight would trouble her afterwards.

As we walked together he told us about other small harmless snakes he'd seen in the wild. When the weather is very dry and very hot in Cape Town, the lore is that they come down from Table Mountain and hide where it's coolest. There were stories of people finding them on the kitchen floor, because they like the coolness of the tiles.

'About so long.' He indicated a foot length with his hands.

'Yeah, right,' Kate said in disgust. 'Pull the other one.'

'They are just as scared of us as we are of them,' Patrick assured her.

Neither Kate, nor I, for that matter, was convinced.

We'd spent most of the time looking at leopards and one, in particular, draped luxuriously along a branch, one forepaw hanging, carefree. Even though they were fenced in, their coats gleamed and their beautiful heads possessed a feral grandeur. Kate had taken a few photographs and made some sketches and Patrick silently glanced at me from time to time, like the animals, alert to every move. Horse! I thought, reminded of the spirited black coat of a neighbour's horse, the nearest thing to a wild animal I'd known as a child. Horses I'd seen at the races with my father ran riderless after a fall. 'Dangerous,' my father warned, following the race with his field glasses. I could only ever see them as beautiful and untamed.

On the way home we stopped for a drink. As the barman collected the empties and took our order Kate disappeared to play pool at the far end of the lounge.

'What about a drive on Friday after work? There's something I want to show you.' Patrick's arm was casually round my shoulder and his thumb inside my collar caressing my skin. 'We can be there and back by midnight?' I needed time to think.

Fortunately Kate returned, a cue in her hand. 'Dad, come on, give me a game?' she said.

'Later on,' he replied. 'We've got to take Eve home.'

'Yeah, right.' Kate looked at me. 'It's a really good place and nobody's waiting. Mind if we stay?' Her red hair was woven into a French plait. She was wearing a yellow sweater and denim dungarees, and she looked younger than she had the afternoon at the cinema.

'No problem,' I said.

Content to stay where I was, every now and then I glimpsed Kate and Patrick across the early evening gloom of the bar, poised over the green baize. My thoughts were interrupted by the click of pool balls against each other or clattering down the shute at the side of the table. Rain teemed against the window and I wondered what it was he wanted to show me on Friday.

EIGHT

On Friday evening we walked together to where the Citroën was parked. The leather seats were springy as we left the motorway and the sky opened out into countryside. It was nightfall as we drove past apple farms and through the small Sussex villages. Seeing fields again did something to calm the fever in my blood. We would have dinner before driving back, Patrick suggested, but my appetite had vanished.

We found ourselves walking along a beach and towards some dunes. The sun was gone and the last light was leaving the sky. A clinker-built sailing boat was tied up at a small jetty. Patrick jumped on board and I followed, as he named parts of the boat and pointed out the depth of the keel in water. A delicious cold breeze caught my hair and salt air blew across my face. The tide was low and the beach empty. We scanned the distance to the car.

The moon rose over the cliff and the sand was pale. Patrick

turned a key in the cabin door, and led me inside. He struck a match and lit a small tilly lamp. The light flickered and wavered, cast a yellow glow. There was a table with seats round it in an alcove, and a sleeping bag along one side. He took a bottle of wine from the satchel on his shoulder, and two glasses.

'I've thought about bringing you here since the day we met. It's my home from home. Very few people come here with me.'

I wondered who the others were. The door was open and the sound of the sea breaking on the pebbles along the shore grew louder. A radio sat on a shelf along with some books. He switched on a small heater and turned the dial on the radio to tune it onto the voice of Nina Simone singing 'My Baby Just Cares For Me'. I was looking at a map of the Channel on the wall when he stood behind me and drew my body close, moving slowly to the music.

'Have you always owned a boat?' I spotted tide-gates and currents on the map, and nestled against his chest.

'Ever since I was six and climbed to the top of the lime tree in my grandmother's garden,' he said dreamily, his arms around my waist, holding me tight against him.

'The leaves filled up like sails?' I said, luxuriating in the heat along my back where our bodies touched.

'I used to hang an old red sheet from the top of a branch. It was my secret place. The thing I love about waking up on a boat is being somewhere new.'

I told him about my mother and her partner, Danny, and the journeys they made in summer.

'That's what I call sailing,' he said, and asked if I'd ever gone with them, his lips to the nape of my neck.

Once as a teenager, I went out into the bay and beyond. When we stopped for the night, we were in sight of the Great Blasket. Single lights glimmered on the island. As I hung over the side, they showed me the bright phosphorescence in the sea and told me the names for different fish. Danny left lines trailing over the sides to see if there would be something to cook for breakfast.

'I'd love to go there with you,' he said. 'Your west coast.'

I smiled at the thought of the Dingle peninsula being mine. The wide crescent of hills embracing a nest of fields running down to the sea, cutting off the north wind on cold days and allowing the land to bask in the heat when it was warm.

I moved across the cabin to sit on the edge of the table and turned towards him. He followed, and traced my eyebrows with his thumb.

'Close your eyes,' he said suddenly.

The boat swayed beneath us. I closed my eyes. The sound of the sea grew louder. The pressure of his kisses on my forehead increased when it came to my lips. The small lamp gave out but we continued kissing. My eyes got used to the dark, the marine lights in the distance and his weight against mine.

'Think about it.' His voice was taut as he unbuttoned his shirt and undressed quickly, and drew me onto the bunk beside him.

'About . . . ?' I felt him hard against me.

'About waking up on the boat with me.'

'That too?' I wanted him inside me, without having to think about the complications, the tiny bead of pleasure in my uterus already taking on a life of its own.

'We can wait. Nothing ever has to happen.'

'You know where that one led us.'

'If you're sure,' he whispered, groping for his jeans in the dark as he searched for something in the pocket. It was a gesture I would become familiar with, but at that moment I relished the seconds it took to find a condom and tear it from its wrapper.

As I slipped off my shoes and began to unbutton my

blouse, Patrick put his hand on mine. 'Let me undress you,' he whispered.

I stood before him in the darkness and he proceeded to unbutton and unclasp until his lips touched my bare skin and his tongue scorched a path to my breasts.

When he finally entered me, we laboured to a rhythm that grew inseparable from the lift and fall of the boat, my body laden one moment, weightless and buoyant the next. The porthole window was faintly lit and from where we lay I counted dark seconds between each shadowy illumination from the shaft of a distant lighthouse. Each time the glass brightened, he was deeper inside and less of me was solid and more was liquid. I lost track of the light and the dark, everything but our mouths and bodies yearning towards a single pulse, and the rocking and crying of the briny sea that swayed and glimmered with starlight.

'Think about it,' he whispered again, as we lay warm together under the sleeping bag, sipping white wine and listening to jazz tunes on the radio.

'Don't think I'd get much sleep.' I slipped from the bunk and felt for my clothes in the dark.

'Where are you going?' he asked sleepily.

'Wouldn't want to give Sue a fright by not coming home.'

Slowly he began to dress too. When we were ready, he took my hand and turned to the door. Once outside he drew a key from his pocket and locked it, as I walked the small jetty to the water's edge and dipped my hands in the cold sea.

'The sea is warmer than my hands.' I held them out to him, shaking the drops away. He took off his coat and drew it round my shoulders and we followed a dark outline of the high tide mark on the strand. Shells crunched under our feet. I told him about times I swam in the small cove on summer evenings with Denis, letting my body slip from a rock into deep water.

'I loved it too,' he said, warming my hands in his. 'At one stage I made the Cape team, under sixteen. It was a chance of getting away from my parents at weekends.'

Every now and then we faltered and slid on sea lace and bladderwrack.

'The English coast is nothing like the Indian Ocean. In South Africa the Atlantic is close to freezing.'

'Same in Ireland,' I said thinking of home.

'You've got the Gulf Stream. In South Africa, it comes straight from the Antarctic.'

And where does the Indian Ocean come from? I wondered. The idea of two oceans lying side by side, one warm and one cold, was a mystery to me. At the point where they meet, round the Cape of Good Hope, where exactly did they become one and was the difference palpable?

When we neared the car, a white curve of foam gleamed below us. Further out, the darkness was a charcoal mist over the sea. He stopped and inhaled deeply. He had drawn up the collar of his jacket and I gave him back his coat as we got into the car. There was a table in the restaurant near an open fire but the kitchen was closed and the waitress offered dessert and coffee.

As he drove us back to the city in the small hours, the trees were blanched in fog. The world felt like the inside of a dream. My head lay against the headrest and my hands cupped Patrick's hand where it lay warm on my lap. The lights of oncoming cars shone on the windscreen.

When I reached the house, it was still. The kettle was hot but there was no sound of anyone up. I was glad to slip upstairs and undress.

NINE

Warm water coursed down my body, over my back and shoulders, and washed away the touch of his hands. I wrapped my hair in a towel, dried my skin and lay under the covers.

When my mother taught me to swim, warm and cold currents swept past as I learned to float. She insisted on swimming lessons in the sea during summer holidays, in pools marked out with rope. The shock of the cold would stop me from thinking about anything else. I'd tread water before swimming to rocks at the mouth of the cove, or I'd crawl on my back far out on an incoming tide. The big lift of the ocean beyond the cove would hold me in its sway. Here and there the water was so clear it was possible to see the sand at the bottom. These stretches were best, and places blue-black with seaweed and rock were to be avoided. Face down on the buoyant surface, I felt weightless.

My mother often sat reading or chatting with friends

when we played in the rock pools in the sun. She would hold out a towel as I ran towards her, and even now I can feel the heat of her skin on my cold wet limbs as she held me close. We towelled and dusted with baby powder and my foot tickled in the palm of her warm hand as she dried between each toe. My hair hanging damp round my shoulders, I'd hand her the brush and ease myself onto her lap. My brother would stop his digging in protest and climb up next to her or try to push me off, his small face scrunched up with fury.

'Let Eve have a rest!' she'd scold.

It was no use. I would have to wait until evening when he was asleep and my mother was tired. Even so she would hold me on her lap by the light of the lamp and read from a story-book until a sentence caught in my head and sleepily I repeated it back to her. Then it was time for bed. She'd lead me upstairs by the hand to my own room where I slipped between the cool sheets to fall fast asleep. What would she think now, my mother?

When I told her I was moving to London, she didn't seem concerned. She shrugged and said that I was old enough to make my own decisions. There was something so detached in the way that she said it that I was stranded. She had no interest in London, or Dublin, for that matter. There was nothing in either place that she needed. There was the boat that spent nine months of the year in dry dock, sometimes in the yard or down on the pier. When school holidays came, the days were spent listening to weather reports and wind speeds. Ever since my brother and I began to work in the summer, she and Danny would head out in the mornings or occasionally make a journey that took two or three days. She never went out in anything above a force five, and always longed for the winds to be light and the days to be fine. The nights when they slept at sea were the ones she loved most. She would talk about the stars and the brightness of the night sky.

In the kitchen, as I cleared slugs from the lettuces, my mother said nothing. It took weeks to tell her, choosing the right words and preparing my defence.

'I've been offered a new job and I really want to say yes but it's in London and Denis . . . ' My words trailed away guiltily.

'He never had time for the city.' She was sitting by the window reading the newspaper and looked up for a moment.

'It would be easier for him to find a job in London than it is for me. The construction industry is booming.'

'Mmmm,' she agreed. 'What are you going to do?'

I drew a chair to where she sat. 'Work with publishers.'

That was when I asked her what she thought and she told me it was my own decision. Outside the window the black cat was curled on the window ledge in the sun. It was late August and the small drills of potatoes, scallions and lettuces ran in neat rows to the bank. There were tomatoes under glass. Beyond the fuchsia hedge was an open field with cattle.

Sometimes when the field flooded, Connor and I used to try to float small wooden rafts, which we assembled from orange boxes. Or we took our bicycles along the path to the wood and came home by road.

She was absorbed in the newspaper again. I suddenly wanted to shout, Now that you have Danny, nobody else really matters. Instead, I looked keenly at her face, paler and softer with age, laughter lines round her eyes deepening to wrinkles, the strands of grey in her hair. This face that I loved had aged without my noticing it, during all those weeks and months I was away in Dublin. She had become used to my absence and receded inside herself to a place I felt excluded from, one that was masked by a wry pragmatism and a calm that recalled little of her exuberant energy and passionate outbursts when Connor and I were children. The focus of her passion had shifted, and though I'd often flinched at its scrutiny, now I somehow missed its passing. I love you, I wanted to say, but the words stayed in my throat.

'You are a mummy person,' one of my school friends said years ago. I nodded in recognition. There in the kitchen I realised how that had changed too, by incendiary moments when circumstances forced their way between us. When a name for that crucible was needed, I conveniently called it Daniel.

When slates came off the roof in a storm my mother found Danny. Some time later, he designed a greenhouse for the back garden.

'Just doodling,' he'd say, showing her the plans.

'I'm not sure I've got the money,' she'd sigh.

'Let me know when you do and we'll make a start.' There was a twinkle in his eye.

He had a flat in Dingle overlooking the park. There was a large living room that stretched from the front to the back of the house, and a high sloping desk in the centre of one room, with the site plans he was working on. There were shelves of books and jars of pencils and unwashed mugs, and photographs that he had taken himself, rock-scapes and shell studies and the patterns of sand on the shore. One taken from the boat showed him hauling in a great fish.

It was his air of being oblivious of his surroundings, his desk strewn with sketches and crayons, and his ability to be lost in the middle of it that struck me at first. Connor and I called him 'Dan Pencils', and I thought of him as an animal that disappears into the ground. Fox or beaver. Months later, on my way home from school, my mother dropped in to let him know she had enough saved for the materials.

'Have a look at the drawings,' he said, handing her a file from an old wooden cabinet. 'If you like, I'll drop in one evening, and we could pool our ideas.' He looked at the three of us and smiled.

Sometime after that news of my father's death came on the telephone, swift as the fall of an axe. I sat down at the kitchen table and got up again, then walked out the back door straight into the screech of the electric saw which had started up at intervals all afternoon. The sound of the blade shearing through wood, then stopping, left a silence that pulsed in the garden, broken only by the song of a bird. Connor was down the road at a friend's house. He knew nothing about our father. It would be hours before he came home. My mother stood with her hand on my shoulder, rubbing it mindlessly until I moved away. She went to speak to Danny in the garden shed. I saw him mop his brow with the back of his hand and disconnect the lead from the saw as I crossed the yard and walked to the horse's field. Clipper was grazing in the corner, and I crossed the grass and stood near, waiting for him to come. He looked up and ambled expectantly towards me. He nuzzled my palm.

'I'm sorry Clip. I forgot to bring something,' I said, my eyes welling up with tears. 'He's gone,' I whispered. 'And I promised I wouldn't let the summer pass without seeing him.'

The horse stood still now, ears pricked at the sound of my voice.

I remembered my father the last time I saw him, extending the crook of his arm and hugging me to his shoulder. 'You should drop in more often,' he called, as I waved goodbye. In my mind's eye I could see Ellen sitting between us, her silent gaze and her awkwardness at my being there. I recalled the crunch of gravel under my feet and the settling of the small leather backpack he had given me for my birthday as I walked away.

For a long moment my head rested on the horse's neck and my forehead grew warm from the contact. When I dropped my hand from his mane and turned to go, he followed me to the gate and whinnied after me.

When I got back to the house, the key was in the lock but Danny was no longer working in the garden and there was no sign of my mother. The electric saw was still on the workbench in the shed, surrounded by a heavy fall of sawdust, and the unplugged extension cable trailed across the floor.

TEN

I felt Irish in London. By naming my difference, Patrick broke the silence around it. He was keen on accents generally, and sometimes asked me to repeat things because he liked how it sounded. His own accent with its strongly enunciated vowels was muted by many years of living in London. He was different too. For me, it meant that his 'Englishness' was less of a threat, just another colour, racially speaking, and not designed to make me inferior.

When the topic of Northern Ireland was raised, I was less sure of my ground. In the office no one spoke of it as part of the United Kingdom. One morning, as we were having a break, a mention of Oliver Cromwell as Lord Protector and a great national leader made me uncomfortable. Carol quoted the dust jacket of the biography she was reading, and at first I thought it was a disinterested remark. And then she said, 'He was very effective. I've always had a soft spot for him. And John Milton.'

'You have?' I said in disbelief. Hearing someone casually praise Cromwell was like listening to a neo-Nazi interview on television.

Carol didn't know about Cromwell's Irish campaign. Or perhaps she had forgotten it. She was saying that he was a visionary and a man of action, the ultimate soldier, a soldier of God. He held the country together at a time of instability.

I was actually beginning to break out in a sweat and was acutely aware that if I spoke, the tone of my voice would sound hot and clammy too. It was much easier to say nothing. But the longer the silence, the harder it became to break it, and the more self-conscious I grew about hearing myself speak.

After listening to a litany of Cromwell's virtues, Patrick looked at me expectantly.

I turned to Carol. 'What about Drogheda?'

'Drog-eed-a?' she repeated.

The name sounded silly on her tongue, the place groggy.

'Drogheda,' I said again. 'Droichead Átha. *Droichead* means "bridge" and *Átha* means "ford" – the ford on the Boyne where the river flows into the sea.'

'Lovely name,' she said blandly, closing the subject.

He looked at her and then at me. 'You were saying?' he asked.

I stammered. 'It happened a long time ago.'

'What did?' he insisted.

'The massacre of about three thousand civilians. It started on September 11, 1649,' I said slowly, my voice growing calmer as I spoke.

Carol got up to pour herself another cup of tea. 'Never knew Cromwell went to Ireland,' she said. 'Patrick's interest in the Irish question is very recent,' she added pointedly.

Doris, the receptionist, and Tony, the designer, exchanged glances.

'Never too old to learn,' Patrick said calmly.

Carol must have sensed that we'd met without her, though I hadn't told her about going to the pictures or the concert weeks earlier. She turned to Adele, and pursed her lips with a faint air of satisfaction that said, I told you so.

Adele looked at me with some sympathy. 'The ferocity of the Irish campaign was legendary.'

Unwittingly perhaps, Carol had raised the Irish issue and I felt stung by it. I was of the same race as those who had planted bombs across the North and in England. She had never been to Ireland, and even if my Irishness was until now overlooked, I was reminded that the country I'd left was not.

My clothes felt too tight and I wanted to leave the room. By becoming involved with Patrick, I'd trespassed a boundary. First it was Kate with prior claims on him, and now Carol. There was Gilly still to meet.

Adele rose and put away her cup. 'If you have time later, we could take a look at a couple of formats that Tony has come up with for the teenage series,' she said to me, signalling Doris and Tony to follow her.

It was my cue to escape but leaving just then smacked too much of cowardice.

Patrick turned on Carol once the others had left. 'Nobody holds a candle to John Donne. How could one possibly like Milton? All that rhetoric and preaching, and as for Cromwell . . .'

'But *Paradise Lost* is so dramatic,' she insisted, 'and so visual in its appeal, like a modern cartoon really.'

'For Godsake hold your tongue . . . ,' Patrick quoted wryly as he collected our cups to place them on the tray.

'And let me love?' Carol murmured demurely, glancing at me.

'Eve came to the pictures with us a couple of Saturdays ago,' Patrick confided, smiling at me.

'You met Katie?' She was astonished.

'It was definitely an event.'

'What did you see?'

'Not the film. Meeting Kate.'

'I must ring her,' she said, letting me know she kept in touch with Kate.

'She'd like that,' Patrick said, with a little too much gusto.

'I'll see you in a few minutes,' I called after her as she left the room.

We were finally alone and standing near enough to touch. It would have been easy to close the gap and hold him but this was the office.

'Don't know much about Irish history,' he apologised.

'Don't know much about South Africa,' I smiled and turned to leave the room.

ELEVEN

Ever since the exchange over Cromwell with Carol and she heard that I had been to the pictures with Patrick there was a coolness in the air between us and a new gusto in her voice when she gave me deadlines and instructions in the office and a distance in mine receiving them.

A day or two later, in conversation over a script, she reminded me that I spoke something called Hiberno-English. After that, I tried to restrain the unruly fluency of my native tongue, as if it were a reflection of looseness in other areas, and heard myself slow down my speech and pronounce words more carefully. As a result, my own diction was stilted as I tripped on a word that came out hampered and that hung in the room between us.

Because we were very busy just then and schedules had to be met, it was easy for both of us to limit contact to times when information had to be exchanged. I made efforts to reach her and deep down I longed to speak openly with her as a friend as the week crawled by. She responded to invitations for coffee or a drink after work by casually putting it on the long finger, and in turn kept letting me know that she was about to meet Patrick to discuss a script or settle queries over permissions. It made me aware that Carol's status in the company as gifted editor was long-standing and her claims on Patrick's attention secure. My tenure would be due for review in a couple of months, and my entanglement with him would hardly be considered an asset.

When I found a card from him among the pages of a typescript I was working on, with the words of Donne's poem, 'The Good-morrow', Carol was sitting at her desk on the other side of the room with her back to me. I scanned Donne's lines and then read his inky handwriting that said:

> Dear Eve, I was checking a quotation for an epigraph when I came across these lines, which we will use for the Mason biography and wondered if you knew the poem? It was a favourite of mine at school. As you may know by now, poetry is not my thing but I make an exception for Donne. You are on my mind most of the time. See you at the weekend? Patrick.

I wanted to dance on the spot. The skylight window was open and the unseasonally warm air for late March lifted the papers on my desk. Carol coughed then and I glanced over my shoulder at her observant back, and quickly placed the card in my bag which was slumped on the floor by my chair.

At home that evening I took out the poem and read it again in the kitchen:

> My face in thine eye, thine in mine appeares,
> And true plain hearts doe in the faces rest,
> Where can we finde two better hemispheares

Without sharpe North, without declining West?

As the poem's candid declaration slowly penetrated a palpable fever grew in my veins. From the kitchen window I noticed that the thundery clouds on the eastern sky were streaked to blood-orange in the fading light. The persistent din of an exultant blackbird drew me into the garden, where the loamy smell of the earth meant spring and I watched two cats circle each other under an Australian palm, one drawing the other on with a scent. Sam and Sue were at the theatre, and would be late getting back.

For the rest of the evening I was restive and impatient to phone him but decided to let the moment settle. Instead, I busied myself by clearing the clutter that had gathered in my room over the winter – magazines and weekend sections of newspapers that accrued on the bookshelf in untidy drifts, old letters and postcards, clothes I'd grown tired of.

When it was all done, I turned out the light in the room and lit the buttery yellow bedside lamp on the small table beside the double bed. So far I had only slept on the boat with Patrick. What would he make of my room? The new spaciousness set off the pale pink and white chequered covers and lace pillows.

Later I lay in the darkness, watching as the lights went out in the windows of a row of houses beyond the back garden, and imagined my hand resting lightly on his left hip as it did the night he slept on the boat and I lay awake watching him. Earlier, as I knelt astride him, he caressed my legs all the way up until I opened for him and drew him inside and he was big and hard driving up into me. I arched my back and pushed out my breasts that were tense and full and he was tormented trying to reach them. I was glad to torment him and eased beyond his grasp, my eyes scanning his face in the darkness below me as he rose higher and my body grew lighter drawing him on as though I were riding on air like a dancer I'd seen in a small theatre. She was balanced on the palm of a hand, stretched several feet from the ground, her body lifted as if she were weightless. It was Patrick who strained beneath me and my faith in his strength and reliability was so complete that I didn't contemplate the possibility of falling; only the thrill of being lifted.

I fell asleep with his arms round my waist. When I woke in the night he was lying on his back, his arms under his head, his whole body so open and surrendered in sleep I lay looking at him for a long time. His breathing was deep and even. His brown hair was tousled and curled slightly on his forehead, in a way that made him look younger and more carefree than he did in the daytime. Already I wanted to shield him from the smallest disappointment.

Something about him was beyond me. Something partly to do with where he came from. As if his country of birth lay dormant within him and, all night, creatures of the veldt – zebra, antelope, lion and lizard – marched south in colonies beneath his skin. He was all the sunny days I'd missed as a child, all the afternoons when my horizon was reduced to a blur of rain on the window. His memory was encoded with the temperatures and felicities of a hemisphere I'd never experienced and that reflected my own, only vaguely in reverse. My cold spring was his endless summer.

As I gazed at his sleeping face it occurred to me that this was how he lived – with a fierce carelessness, holding nothing back, trusting like a child. If things didn't work out, he'd be capable of utter desolation. It was that very transparency of feeling I found so compelling. I agreed to things I hadn't meant to and found myself saying things I'd never said to anyone before, so that speaking to him was like thinking aloud. That was how he was able to reach across the barriers of age, as if he was exempt from its limits, like Oisín come to Tír na nÓg. I had been struck by the sheer improbability of Niamh's desire to draw a total stranger away from kith and kin, across meadow and sea to a land of eternal youth.

At heart I was no romantic and there was no evil spell I wished to be delivered of. I did not cause Patrick to forfeit his world, but our horizons were northern all the same, more mine than his, and the sense of trespass when we met was exciting and vaguely treacherous.

It was very late and my room was chilly. I switched on the lamp to rearrange the pillows and smooth the duvet, in the hope that an orderly bed would incline me to sleep.

As a child, I was often sent upstairs to tidy and shake out the quilts. I'd open the windows and shake the covers over the window ledge, or leave them hanging while I lay on my bed reading. A book I loved was about the circus and I dreamed of walking the tightrope and flying the trapeze. At that age I was fearless and confident and blind to consequences, as Patrick seemed now. One day I would take him to sleep with me in that room. I'd be high in the air in the darkness, balancing, my arms spread like wings.

TWELVE

My hesitant feet carried me through the reception area and down the corridor and I reminded myself to breathe when I reached his door. He was alone and walked round the table to meet me. His hands remained by his sides. All the air seemed to have deserted my lungs. I picked up the keys on his desk and handed them to him.

'Let's break for lunch? It's almost that time. Would you like to come back to the house with me?' he said.

I looked at my watch. There was a meeting scheduled with Carol for the afternoon.

'It's only five minutes away,' Patrick assured me, taking my elbow as we left the room and headed downstairs to walk to his car. Soon we were heading south on the Finchley Road, and my heart was beginning to race. He was humming the tune of Lily Marlene.

Did he often take women home, pointing out local landmarks as he did now? White cumulus clouds hung across the sky but the sun was shining and daffodils were flowering in front lawns and the last primroses were in window boxes. The car turned into quieter streets, before pulling into the car park of a terraced house.

He led me in through the hallway to a living room that looked out on the garden. He opened the patio door and offered coffee or juice.

'Both,' I decided, heading into the lawn, between apple trees to one side and a small magnolia on the other. Low privet hedges ran down on either side. At the far end the garden was wilder, and rushes sprouted up through the tufts of grass. The boundary between it and a neighbour's garden was a trench of water, which trickled like the streams at home.

Patrick was standing in the patio with two glasses and as I walked back to him he gave me one and returned to the living room, which had many photographs and interesting objects. Stones, shells, pieces of sculpted wood. Shelves of books. A rack or two of CDs. He placed a conch shell in my hands.

'I found the card you sent me.' I smiled, placing the mouth of the seashell to my ear.

'And you haven't run away,' he noted happily.

My own ear listening was echoed back to me in whispers of the seabed. Distant and indistinct.

'Not yet,' I teased. 'I feel as if I'm walking on eggs.'

He indicated a chair and we moved to the table to sit down, the corner between us, and I took off my jacket.

'Carol's feathers are ruffled and I'll speak to her. She's fond of Kate too. Once people accept us as a couple, it'll get easier,' he reasoned, making light of it.

We were not a couple, then, if the acceptance of others was to be taken into account. I held my peace. Not like when I met Denis in Dublin and started going out with him. Within a month we were living together. There was nothing easy about Patrick and myself. I'd seen him too often around others to assume any claims on him. He clasped his hands behind his head and regarded me.

'What?' I asked, looking at him. Perhaps I wanted to get my own back, and that's why I sounded like the ice queen. 'I like it when we sleep together. That's all.'

Now he was annoyed. 'It can't be all.'

'Isn't it enough for now? Better to assume nothing lasts . . . than to start out assuming it does and spend half a lifetime crying over it?' Why could I not let him know how I really felt? My job was hanging in the balance, Carol was barely speaking to me, and I was scared of being let down.

'How romantic of you.' He got up and went to the kitchen. 'Would you like a cheese sandwich?'

'If I expect the worst every now and then, life takes me by surprise. Meeting you was that.'

'It's brave of you to speak in that way, and I don't believe a word of it,' he said gently, coming back with some bread and cheese on a board, along with some butter, and setting a plate for each of us. His look was a challenge.

At the sound of his words a tear welled up at the corner of my eye, and I brushed it quickly away.

'See, I think I'm right after all,' he noted.

I smiled hesitantly. 'Kisses make it better,' I said, echoing something my mother used to say when I was a child and fell, grazing my knee or my hand.

He leaned across and placed his lips to my cheekbone and then rubbed his forehead against mine. 'You remind me of someone called Ellie. She grew up next door and became my girlfriend for a couple of years. I used to think we'd always be together.' He smiled and waited for my reaction.

'Like Denis and myself.'

He nodded. 'Childhood sweethearts. Her family was Jewish,' Patrick continued. 'I was in love with her. Her father was interested in motorbikes, as a hobby. He had a

Harley. He used to let me ride it sometimes. Her brother Jamie was my best friend growing up.'

'Sue's got a brother named James,' I said.

'Have you met him?' Patrick asked.

'Not for years. We were in school together. He's Denis's older brother. We're going to meet him one Saturday for a picnic.'

'I see,' Patrick said vaguely. 'Anyway, it ended rather badly.'

'Ellie saw you with somebody else.' I was fishing.

He looked troubled. 'There was nobody else. We were too young. Ellie had to be home by midnight, even at weekends. For something to do, I went to a nightclub with the others.'

'So she was right,' I decided.

He looked guarded and amused at the same time. 'Man, did I pay for it. You remind me of her.'

I didn't want to be like anyone else, especially not someone that he was unfaithful to.

'Ellie? Whatever picture you have of me, I know I'm not that person.' The idea that it wasn't me but someone else he cared for was infuriating. I suddenly hated this Ellie.

He frowned and shook his head. 'It's not in that way you remind me of her. I haven't felt this way for a long time.'

'What about Gilly?' I didn't want him to have felt that way about anyone else, even if it was twenty years ago, and hadn't he loved his wife? He had been around far too long.

'With Gilly, at least we had our chance to work things out. With Ellie, I was very attracted to her and involved when we split up. It felt like an open wound.'

Had I left Denis feeling that way? 'You're the father's daughter,' he'd said, the morning I left the flat.

Patrick started to clear away the food. I followed him into the kitchen and buttered a bread roll.

'I want to get serious with you,' he warned, resting his hip against the worktop. 'I'll try hard not to fuck up.'

'You being a mere mortal? What's wrong with fucking up every now and again?'

I wiped the back of my hand across my mouth to clear away the breadcrumbs and laughed with him then, and suggested that once he came to know me better, he would be disappointed. My insides were in turmoil again. Did he think I was there just for play, and to run away at the sight of trouble?

He reached out a hand and I took it and he drew me towards him until my weight was resting against him.

'How do I look?' I asked, running my hand over my cheeks that felt hot and my hair that was loosened from its clasp.

'Show me.' He turned me round to check my clothes and hair. 'If I say what I think, you mightn't like it. See how complicated things are,' he protested. 'So what if I just say this?' He took my face in his hands and kissed me. His palm rested on my collarbone.

I drew away from the hungry insistence of his mouth and took his hand and turned, heading for the door. In the car he started the engine and reversed onto the road. The car moved into the traffic, and big drops of rain hit the bonnet.

We drove in silence through the downpour, so heavy that the wipers were slowed by the weight of water on the windscreen. Patrick switched on the radio news and rested a hand on my knee. We were wedged between red buses and black taxis, all brought to a snail's pace by the rain.

When he parked on a street next to the office, the rain was still falling heavily and we kissed again until the weather cleared and then ran to the side door, both late for our meetings.

THIRTEEN

Clipper used to roll on his back in the field when he was happy. One day I watched him rolling in the paddock, hoofs in the air and then getting up and galloping around the field.

'Is something wrong with him?' I asked my father.

'Far from it,' he replied.

'But his coat's all muddy now.'

'Never mind, that's how he likes it. It'll dry off and you can brush him down, or give it a scrub later on.'

I liked the feel of his coat when it shone. The paddock was broken by his hoofs and a muddy path ran round the grassy edge of the field.

Once when friends of Connor came to play, they painted their foreheads and cheeks with mud. I sat with them, hunkered in the corner of the paddock, and watched as they dug their hands into the earth. It was summer and they took their T-shirts off and encouraged me to do the same. They were pretending to be warriors hiding in the trees, and good camouflage was necessary. They rubbed mud on each other and pulled leaves from the branches of an ash tree to trail from their waists.

'We'll help you,' Mark offered, holding up hands caked in dirt. 'You can be our prisoner.'

And so I took off a broderie anglaise bodice and lay down, feeling the soft cold slide of the mud beneath my skin. I was just twelve and already my breasts were beginning to form. The boys stood and stared. With an index finger, I rubbed clay around one nipple and then the other. Connor started to rub his mucky palm gingerly over my stomach. The others took their cue from him and started to paint me to the waist. I watched the boys as they revelled in their work, paying more attention to my breasts than anything else. I pulled my hair into a band and daubed my face with clay. That way, no one would recognise me at a quick glance.

'Tie her hands, and put her in the cubby in the trees,' Mark ordered, and I rolled over on my stomach to let them tie my hands with a short piece of twine. Under the tree the air was cool and the light dappled. The fretted bark bore into my skin as I leaned against it. Then a voice called, 'Mark! Shane!' An older sister had come to collect them.

'Run!' Shane shouted, and they dropped from the branches and raced off in the direction of the stream.

'I'll be there in a minute,' I called back to the girl. 'Wait for me in the kitchen.'

It was difficult to cross the wire fence with hands behind my back, but I managed it and walked across the field to the others like a proud hostage queen, my skirts trailing, the mud beginning to cake and dry to a pale colour.

'You're in trouble now!' Connor shouted. 'We're all in trouble. Why didn't you run?'

In the kitchen my mother treated me to a rare silence.

'Are you taking after him?' she spat, when she finally did open her mouth.

'After who?' I challenged, knowing that *he* and *him* referred to my father.

She didn't answer and instead handed me an old baby bath now used for steeping woollens, and a box of Surf.

'At least he's happy,' I snapped, 'and doesn't spend his life giving out to people.'

'Clean up that mess and wash every one of those filthy clothes.' Her anger hardened, like molten metal turning solid.

I knelt over the small bath and turned on both bathroom taps, and added a generous measure of washing powder. My fingers grew red and raw in the water as the detergent seared my hands.

The sight of mud on our faces or bodies would not normally have incensed my mother. Because the boys were younger, she assumed that I was ringleader. Already there were girls in my class with boyfriends and older girls and boys who smoked and kissed in the bus shelters, or down at the bottom of the playing fields, furtively huddled together.

The girl who left school a couple of years before to have a baby just before her Leaving Cert was Ellen Hanley. For a week it was the talk of the place. My mother taught science to the class and was particularly troubled to 'lose' a conscientious student, especially one so close to the family. Months before, Ellen had left the lab several mornings complaining of weakness.

She stayed back after class one day and told my mother that she would keep her baby and that her parents would look after her. In class she had been diffident and hardworking, like she was when she looked after us, and my mother stared at her in shock, blind until now to the pallor of her face and the burgeoning contours of her body. It was clear that she wouldn't be sitting her exams and her ambition to study medicine was now more dream than possibility.

When I heard, I imagined her with a baby in her arms in the green school uniform. She was talked about in whispers – she was 'up the pole', had a 'bun in the oven'. She was called an 'eejit' by the streetwise and a 'slut' by adults who didn't know her.

'Why are you so cross?' I asked my mother one evening when she was folding towels and bed linen she'd taken from the tumble dryer.

'She didn't use her brains.' She handed me the corners of a sheet and pulled it straight along the length before we doubled it again. She worked quickly and tugged the folded ends from my grasp.

'Maybe she's happy? She might have wanted a baby.'

'The boyfriend isn't able to support her.' She ran her hand over the sheet to smooth away the creases.

'How do you know?' At that moment I hated her certainty.

My mother extended another sheet to fold. 'Because I do,' she said angrily.

'You think you do, but you don't,' I insisted, drawing the corners together. Ellen was friendly with several of the boys in her class. She'd told me the names of the ones she liked but her boyfriend was a couple of years older.

'All right so,' I said, smoothing the folded corners of a sheet.

'If you know so much, who is the father?' she quizzed, hoping to call my bluff.

My mother glared and said nothing more. Her exasperation, I assumed then, was fuelled by her desire to see the girls in her class do well, even outshine the boys.

'Tom Kearney. He works at home in the garage,' I conceded, aware that she disliked my knowing so much.

'It reduces her options,' she said finally. 'Ellen Hanley of all people. The world was at her feet. If it was one of those lassies from the town, I wouldn't mind.'

Ellen's disgrace was somehow connected to my own, as if by crossing a line, we were similar in our desire to be at one with the earth itself. The sense of indictment that hung in the air ensured that I would never follow in her footsteps, or, at least, not as long as my mother could help it.

FOURTEEN

I came across Kate sitting in the tearoom one evening as I was about to leave work. She was wrapped in a green padded jacket, her legs stretched in front of her, her satchel under her elbow. Her hair was hidden beneath her pink woollen hat, but her freckled face was unmistakable. She looked up as I walked through and then after a flicker of recognition awkwardly looked at the floor. I walked towards her.

'Hi there!' I said. 'Are you meeting your dad?'

'That was the plan. I've been here since five. I came straight from school.'

'Let's go and see Doris.'

'No thanks,' she said glumly. 'I'll wait for Carol. She usually knows where he is.' She eyed the floor.

'I'll see what I can find out,' I offered. 'Carol is working at home today.'

She shrugged.

We went downstairs to Doris's office on the ground floor. She was a warm woman who seemed to keep the house running.

'Patrick?' I asked. 'His daughter's been waiting for him.'

She picked up the appointment book and ran through the list. 'Sorry, love, nothing here. Come to think of it, I don't remember seeing him today.' She looked at me over her spectacles. 'Let's see.' She tried several extensions but wasn't able to trace him. 'Want to try his home?' She keyed the number and handed me the receiver.

I was about to protest when a familiar voice spoke on the line. It was Carol. She occasionally worked with Patrick at her place. But here she was at Patrick's.

I explained that Kate was in the office and needed to speak to her father. When he came on the line, he sounded flustered and apologised for his lateness. He hadn't been feeling well and Carol had called with him for some help with an author's stubborn responses to an edit she'd done. He asked if I would stay with Kate until he got to the office and I handed her the receiver.

Kate suggested we wait for him at a patisserie and teashop on Finchley Road, her glance checking with me as she spoke to her father. I nodded and she arranged to meet there around six.

As we walked towards the café, Kate's awkwardness was replaced by curiosity.

'Is Carol at *our* house then? She usually visits when I'm at home,' she mused. 'Is she working with Dad?'

I nodded as two lanes of traffic roared by. He was unwell, I told her.

'Then he should be in bed and not trying to work,' she declared. 'If I'm not feeling well, he insists that I go to bed.'

We'd reached a pedestrian crossing and she pushed the button on the lights. I smiled at her irritation. Surely Carol could have waited until he was back at work to see him?

The café was warm and the Spring movement of Vivaldi's *The Four Seasons* was playing in the background.

'Thanks,' she conceded, sipping her chocolate milkshake. 'If you hadn't shown up . . . '

'He was about to ring the office to speak to you,' I said to reassure her.

'I didn't believe him, you know, when he said he worked with you.' She stirred her milkshake thoughtfully and avoided my eyes.

'Why not?' I asked.

'He pretends it's work so that I won't get mad and tell Mum. You don't look like work,' she said.

I sipped my tea. 'You're right. I'm not just work,' I admitted. Why should I lie to her?

Kate's eyes widened. She was incredulous.

'Dad's ancient. You can't be serious.'

'I'm afraid I am.' I smiled.

She glanced round at the other tables. Two elderly women in sable coats were sitting within earshot. One turned slowly to Kate and smiled. Under the pale skin of her face, frail as tissue paper, the rich hues of fur glistened luxuriously. Kate averted her eyes quickly and turned back to me.

'I prefer boys my own age. Older guys are sleaze bags.' She fiddled with her straw. 'Mum told me to always stick with people my own age.' She stirred the chocolate residue at the bottom of the glass and looked at me impishly, waiting for an answer.

'Your mum is right.'

'So why don't you stick with people *your* own age? Don't you know any?'

'Of course,' I said.

'Isn't there one you want to go out with?'

'Not really . . . ' I was amused by Kate's questions.

'I'm thirteen. What age are you?' She was persistent.

'Twice that,' I said, speaking from the dock.

'You're closer in age to me than to Dad,' she pointed out. 'If you were seeing someone eighteen years younger they would be eight. Men don't usually go out with older people. That's because they like to be in charge and they only care about looks.' She rested her chin on her fist and considered the situation.

I admired her fierce possessiveness rationalised as principle. 'Do you think being a father changed him?'

Kate's face told me that the question made no sense. 'How would I know?' she puzzled. 'He's my father.'

'There was a time when he wasn't a father.'

Kate's shrug insisted that the world began with her birth. She was unable to imagine her parents without her or their world before she was born. Why was I asking such a silly question?

It was important to me that Patrick liked being a parent and had chosen to stay in close contact with Kate after his break-up with Gilly. I had believed that Dad left my mother because of Connor and myself, as he rarely saw us afterwards. Separation for Patrick could have meant giving up on his daughter as well, but he hadn't abandoned Kate.

'I preferred it when I saw him every day,' she admitted. 'If something bad happens and he's not there . . . ' She looked away stoically.

'I'm sure he misses you most at those times too.'

'I like going to his house and spending the weekends with him on my own.' She folded her arms moodily on the table. 'I have two homes, two beds and two rooms of my own, completely different from each other. I even have two toothbrushes,' she added.

It seemed that being the centre of attention for each separate parent wasn't a particular dilemma for Kate at the moment. It was double the love rather than being split in two.

'Have you . . . ' A half-smile formed on her lips but her eyes were veiled. 'Have you . . . and Dad . . . you know?' Her voice was a whisper.

I smiled, remembering how she'd asked before. She was bashful all of a sudden and leaned back in her chair, her feet curled around the front legs, her eyes now on my face.

I looked at her and silently assented, afraid I'd already given away too much.

She smiled in the way that she might for a camera. It was a mask and beneath it, this new knowledge was troubling. 'Thanks for the chocolate,' she said finally.

The café was humming and a young man placed a hand on the extra chair at our table and asked if it was free. Kate indicated that it was.

'Thanks for your company,' I said, trying to meet her eye.

She was watching the door when Patrick arrived and she tipped backwards on her chair, awkwardly recovering herself as he walked towards us.

'You two seem to be having a good time.' He looked from Kate to myself. She smiled, but beneath the smile her face was strained. 'Very sorry for being so late,' he said, giving her a hug.

I got up to pay at the cash desk.

'Here, Kate,' he said, handing her the keys. 'I'll be along in a second.'

She curled her fingers around the keys and waved at me uncertainly before leaving the café. Outside, I saw her in the car, examining her face in the mirror and bending forward to tune the radio. I wished that Patrick hadn't turned up when he did.

'Carol has a really difficult client at the moment,' Patrick was saying. 'Refuses to make changes, even basic ones. We can't publish the book without being able to stand over it. We'd agreed to meet today, and when I wasn't coming in, she decided to drop up to the house. It was a chance to bring her up to date on what's happening with us,' he added.

I decided that Carol's business with Patrick was her own. From overhearing phone conversations in the office with the author, I knew from the tone of Carol's voice that it was an uphill battle.

'Kate's been asking questions about us,' I said, as we walked to the car. 'She might need to talk about it.'

He met my eyes and agreed. 'You've told her?'

'I hope I haven't said too much,' I warned and then asked him if he was free on Saturday.

'It's my turn, but Kate's staying with a friend, as far as I remember. She's been missing out on sleep-overs.' He ran a hand along my arm and smiled. 'Where are you taking me?'

'Sam and Sue are going away for the weekend,' I said. 'We'll have the house to ourselves.'

'See you Saturday, then,' he replied, as we reached the car.

FIFTEEN

In the afternoon light of that north-facing kitchen it felt as if he were a trespasser from another land. I sat on his lap as we sipped wine, and his palm covered my breast. The buttons of a madonna blue shirt I was wearing were open at the front. While we kissed I could feel his penis stiffen and the muscles of his thighs flex against my weight. I knew that sooner or later I would lead him past the coats in the hall, upstairs to the shadowy bedroom, where the wooden lattice blinds were drawn and sunlight poured through the frame.

That first time in my room he stood with his back to the window, his face in shadow.

'It's been a long time,' he murmured.

It was over a week since we had slept on the boat.

'Waking out there was fun.' My fingers traced the contours of his face. 'I missed you too.'

'I wasn't thinking of the boat just now.'

As he turned to slip the blouse off my shoulder, I could see that his face was troubled. It gave me the feeling that his darkness was beyond me and unfathomable.

I undressed slowly, took his hand and led him towards the bed. We lay on top of the covers. His hands moved along my collarbone and round my breasts, his fingertips reading my skin.

It was then he told me about the nanny, who looked after him before he started school. Her name was Bhinta. She taught him to read and to love stories.

'Bhinta would light a candle and switch off the light and her eyes grew even bigger in the dark. Like your eyes are now.' He smiled, his thumb caressing the hollow at the middle of my collarbone.

'What age was she?' I tried to hold still beneath his hand. On the ceiling a grid of light cast by the window shimmered like water as if the wind were rippling through it.

'Mid-twenties. She had a son of her own in the townships, younger than me, raised by his grandmother. I met Kuli, Bhinta's son, when he came to the house one afternoon. His father was working nearby,' Patrick explained, resting his head on the pillow and stretching flat beside me. 'We swore sacred war on the English boys at the end of our road.'

'Your mother found out?' I could see where it was leading.

'That we started it.'

I knew that Patrick's mother campaigned against apartheid and was a member of the ANC. Seeing her son wage war on his white school friends was not exactly what she'd planned.

'Bhinta was given the sack. I never saw her again. If it's possible to be in love with someone at five years of age, then I was.'

'Think of me as the first. All the other loves are tributaries of this one,' I said gently, wanting to comfort, and running my palm over his chest.

'Doing it for the first time?' he whispered.

'When was that?' I asked, needing to know of his experience.

'I was sixteen and she was twice my age,' he answered slowly. 'She took me inside her and I came too quickly and wanted to try it again.'

'And?' I started to unbutton Patrick's shirt and found the buckle of his belt and opened it. He undressed and we lay under the covers.

'I asked her to teach me, but she only offered to take me home, told me to go back to school if I needed lessons.' He laughed and brushed his hair from his forehead. I leaned down and ran my tongue along his penis.

'Surprise me,' he whispered.

From the street I could hear the afternoon sounds of traffic, and a blackbird's song rose at intervals. The scrape of a button on the floor when his shirt fell off the bed disturbed the quiet in the room, and the rhythm of Patrick's breathing when he finally came.

'I'm all yours,' he said, propping himself on an elbow and smiling down. 'If you're free next Saturday, come with me to the Tate. There's something I want to show you.'

When I pressed him for details, he was enigmatic. I didn't like going to galleries on summer days and said as much but was glad of the arrangement to meet.

'I panic sometimes.'

I hadn't intended saying it, but when we parted, we didn't always make an arrangement to meet again. Even though we saw less of each other at work, there was a tacit understanding that we would meet there. The uncertainty was both tantalising and agonising.

'Panic?' There was incomprehension in his voice.

The idea that he would vanish into thin air or that something might happen to prevent us meeting came from a different place in my life.

'It's not to do with now,' I said quietly.

'It's all right,' he whispered, taking me in his arms again. 'Let's stay here for the afternoon.' He pulled me close.

'What if the doorbell rings?' I asked.

'We won't answer it.' His voice was under the covers and his head lay on my crotch.

'What if it's Sue?'

'She must have her own key.'

'She might pop her head round the door.'

'I'll explain that you've passed out with pleasure,' he said, tickling me.

It is how I remember Saturdays. Patrick arriving at midday with rain on the shoulders of his leather jacket, eager for touch. He was usually up early to finish work or out and about doing chores before he came to me, smelling of the real world. We went to bed for the afternoon or for a frantic hour if Kate was staying for the weekend and had gone to see a friend. Every second week there was time to fall asleep and wake up together. In the early evening we went for a meal or to see a film, returning to the room later.

Sam and Sue were often away overnight, so it was weeks later when Sue met Patrick for the first time. She had just arrived home as he was leaving. We stood in the hallway. She extended a cursory hand and was about to turn away again.

'Congratulations.' He noticed her pregnancy.

'It's a long haul.' She looked at him cautiously.

'It's a miracle,' he insisted.

She was stopped in her tracks, surprised at the familiar nature of his attention. 'You think so?'

'Can't think of anything else like it in creation.'

I was amused at her dubious expression and his solemnity.

'Well it is' – he turned to me – 'I suppose flight is too, even if it can be explained aerodynamically, and the earth's rotation round the sun. There's gravity, of course. Still, I think birth is the greatest.'

I smiled at Sue, who was pale and clearly tired from being on her feet.

She sighed. 'I feel like an old cow.'

'Bears give birth in their sleep,' he said.

'They do?' Sue was sceptical. 'I thought I knew my stuff when it came to this.'

'Sue's a paediatrician,' I explained.

'They hibernate for the winter,' Patrick continued, 'and when they wake up four months later their cubs have been born. While the mother is asleep, the cub eats away the umbilical cord when it gets hungry.'

'Any chance I could turn into a bear?'

They both laughed.

'I hope you don't mind me coming and going. It's a lovely house,' he said, and I watched as his charm worked on Sue.

'That's for Eve to decide,' Sue assured us. 'Sam's on call so much we're glad to have someone else staying here.'

'How many months to go?' Patrick asked.

'Early August.' Sue sounded like it couldn't come fast enough.

'I'm sure you'd like to take the weight off your feet,' he said warmly, taking his leave of her and turning to me.

As he followed me to the gate, he mused, 'I've always found pregnant women irresistible.'

Pregnancy was usually blamed for women losing their shape. That such a loss might proclaim instead ultimate feminine charm was at some objective level just.

SIXTEEN

One evening my mother was going down to the shore to collect seaweed for the garden. It was a job she liked help with, which involved clambering over stones in wellies and hauling great bunches of bladderwrack to the trailer, and I was always happy to go with her. When I went out to the yard, she was sitting in the blue station wagon with Danny. The engine was already running and she called to me that they would be back in about an hour. I was surprised because it was time for him to go home.

They took much longer than an hour and Connor was hungry. We helped ourselves to several bowls of cereal, and then walked to the village to rent a video. By the time we got back, a soft summer rain had turned the fields into fog.

When she came home, she stood in the doorway in an old raincoat, her hair filmed with mist and her face paler than usual. She was soaked to the skin and her eyes shone.

'Where were you?' I asked in surprise, but she just made a

face and said that they had gone for a walk on the strand.

'In the rain?'

'It was just a mist and the tide was out. We got a bit lost.' She smiled.

'You were gone ages,' I said, looking at her as she shook off her coat and hung it in the hallway.

'We're both starving. I've invited Danny to stay for supper.'

'You have? It's after nine o'clock,' I said.

'So it is,' she answered with a deep sigh.

'Connor and I have eaten. Don't worry about us.'

'I need a few minutes to tidy up. Will you find the good tablecloth and wash the salad for me?' she asked, running up stairs.

'What about Connor? Why can't he do it? So far he's done nothing today.'

'Eve,' she called, 'not now. Please, before Danny comes. I'll make it up to you.'

I went to the garden and picked some fresh lettuce and scallions, annoyed that my mother had left us so long on our own. I added as many coloured vegetables as I could find and left them ready for her, and decided to sulk in front of the TV. Why was Danny coming back at this hour?

'You're a darling,' she said, when she returned to the kitchen. It wasn't a word she often used. She was wearing a good blouse, a linen skirt and her only pair of high heels. Her face was still pale and her eyes bright and she checked her appearance in the hall mirror.

'Mum, why are you all dressed up?' I said in consternation. She was breathless from hurrying.

'Danny's gone home to change,' she said. 'He'll be back in a minute. Here, chop this and look lively.' She handed me the onion on a chopping board, along with some garlic.

'I hate chopping onions,' I protested.

'Please. I don't want to look as if I've been crying,' she coaxed.

Suddenly he was standing in the doorway with a great bunch of orange blossom. He must have parked round the side of the house because I didn't hear the car drawing up or notice the headlights. He was wearing a tweed jacket over a casual shirt and jeans, and looked more or less as he always did. My mother blushed and took the knife from my hand. We both stared at him, wordless.

'Here. Let me?' he said, handing her the flowers and taking the chopping knife from her. He proceeded to slice the onion neatly. I looked on with folded arms. My mother disappeared to find a vase. 'The trick is to hold it together,' he said, expertly dicing the translucent layers.

'Doesn't it sting your eyes?' I asked.

'Run cold water for a minute, and I'll be fine.'

My mother returned with the flowers in a vase, which she filled with water at the kitchen sink. The cool sweet scent was a new presence in the room. I left the cold tap running for Danny.

'It's my favourite,' my mother said to him. 'Where did you find orange blossom at this hour of the night?'

He looked at her with an air of secrecy. They both laughed and my mother set the vase in the middle of the table.

'If you hang around here, I might ask you to chop another onion,' Danny said to me.

I stuck out my tongue at him and went to the sitting room, where Connor was watching the film.

'What's happening in the kitchen? Is Mum making us food?' Connor said, as he stretched and switched off the video with the remote control.

'Danny's here,' I said.

'Still?' Connor asked.

'He's just arrived,' I said, lowering my voice.

'But he's been here all day,' Connor complained. 'Is she cooking us supper or what?'

'I told her we were fine.'

'What do you mean, fine? I'm hungry,' Connor said, standing up and striding into the kitchen. I switched on the old valve radio and lowered the volume and watched his progress through the open door. The sky was slate grey in the window, but the rain had stopped.

'Why are we having a party?' Connor asked, as Danny uncorked a bottle of red wine. My mother was frying steak in the pan.

'Great,' Connor said, standing at her elbow. 'Will I get the tomato sauce?'

'I thought you were fed,' she said.

'Nobody cooked for me,' Connor moaned, looking at the table set for two. 'Where am I sitting?' He chose one of the places and sat down. 'Can I light the candle like we do at Christmas?' he asked and went to get the matches.

'That would be lovely,' she said, and called to me, 'Eve, why are you sitting in the gloom? Come here.'

'Not unless I can have a glass of wine,' I demanded, as I wandered into the kitchen.

Danny handed my mother a glass of red wine. She tasted it and he took the glass from her hand and sipped it too.

'Is it all right?' she asked, looking into his eyes.

'It's more than all right,' he said softly. 'Let Eve taste it.'

'She's barely fifteen,' my mother grumbled.

'Melanie,' he appealed, 'show me where the glasses are kept.' He had a certain way of saying her name I heard that night for the first time, as if she were a different person from the one I knew.

Connor reappeared like an altar boy with a lighted candle, and Danny poured some wine into a lemonade glass for me.

'Sip it slowly,' he whispered, handing it to me. 'Otherwise, we're both in trouble.' And turning to Connor, he said,

'Thanks. Now be a good boy and set another place.'

He obeyed without a word and I slipped upstairs with my wine while the going was good.

About half an hour later I could hear Connor's protest. 'It's the weekend,' he complained, climbing the stairs. 'Danny's not gone home from work yet. Why can't I stay up until he goes?'

'You can leave the light on,' my mother said, trying to placate him.

I lay in bed listening to Connor banging about in the bathroom, pretending to wash and brush his teeth.

Much later I heard Danny laughing heartily in the yard and my mother whispering. The sky had cleared and the moon was bright. I lay awake for a long time in the darkness, waiting for the familiar sound of her step on the stairs, and finally dozed off.

The radio woke me. The words of the song rang clear in the stillness. 'I've got you under my skin. I've got you deep in the heart of me.' The voice of Frank Sinatra. My mother was sitting up late, maybe dancing to the music. I looked at my watch. It was almost two. A slant of light from the sitting room shone in the landing.

SEVENTEEN

When we went to the Tate, the gallery was quiet as we climbed the steps. Patrick held my hand loosely in his. The other rested on the strap of a leather bag, slung over his shoulder, which held food for a picnic and a camera. His hair was much shorter, cropped to the back of his head. He looked altogether lighter, as if he had shed weight.

'There's one in particular,' he said, steering me past many of the paintings. 'But we have time to see everything.'

We walked through one room and turned a corner. And there was Bonnard's painting of a young woman, standing at a mirror, her back turned. The image of the body shone from a milky wash of white, giving the impression of skin that was luminous. Her hair was wound in a soft coil at the back of her head. Delicate curves of shoulder and buttock, calf and ankle held my eye. The woman blurred into the veiled abstract quality of the brushwork.

'Maybe she didn't want to be painted?' I pondered, taking in the moment of privacy that we'd encroached upon.

'He captures her body at its most beautiful, before it changes. See the mirror, and the suggestion of a face.'

We were looking at a painted woman engaged in the act of looking at her own face.

'He'll find other beautiful bodies. Isn't that what artists do?' I protested.

Patrick threw me a guarded look. 'See how white the light is.' He nudged me casually. 'In fact, Bonnard hardly ever painted anyone else.'

'Why not?'

'The woman who inspired him became his wife. She forbade it, as far as I know.'

'What a pity!' The idea of having to paint the same person over and over again struck me as tyranny.

'You think so?' he asked, amused.

'Sure,' I said. 'How can looking be imprisoned in that way?'

'Just now you complained that artists . . . '

'If she had to forbid him, what's the point? Anyway, just because he paints someone, doesn't mean he has to fall in love.'

'It's the first step,' Patrick answered. 'Perhaps he wouldn't have used so many interesting angles, or painted the same thing in different moods if he hadn't been so confined . . . '

'Still,' I argued, 'it must have been oppressive.'

Around us, the walls were hung with paintings of interiors. We looked at them in silence and moved on to the next room.

I imagined the future stretched out before us and realised I was beginning to assume that he would always be in my life. Even if I went to the ends of the earth without him, he would be there as close to me as my own breath. When I made my way around London alone, and he was away for the weekend with Kate, or on the boat at Rye, or sitting in a bar with other friends, I got the feeling sometimes that he was just at my shoulder. I had never reached the stage in a relationship where I would want to be with one person for the rest of my life. Yet in the space of a few months, that's how I felt about Patrick.

As I looked at the canvasses I began to see confinement in the work of this painter. His windows and open doors placed the viewer on the threshold of another world. It was as if Bonnard were constantly striking a balance between an interior and an exterior vista. I stopped at a painting of an empty room looking out on a summer garden, ochre and reds creating an atmosphere of molten heat.

'I want to take you,' he whispered, 'to the hot country. It's partly why I wanted you to see this.'

The hot country was how he and Kate referred to South Africa.

'You do?' I said, feeling the sudden lift of a big wave against my ribcage. 'This is France,' I said awkwardly, eyeing another picture of an abandoned dining table.

'After the Cape, no other hot country will do. Wait until you see,' he said, taking a couple of steps forward to look at something in detail.

Images of Africa came to mind, clusters of children at school lessons under trees, or gaunt, breastfeeding mothers standing in line at a clinic. Wounded blacks on dusty streets, their blood the same shocking red as my own. Would I really like to go there? There would be nothing like the ditches that ran around small fields everywhere at home, trickling with streams, no stone walls either, with gaps for sheep that were once good for hide-and-seek. Instead, the bush, stretching for miles and miles and the blue vastness of the sky. The affluent cities and the shabby townships. The shame of being white. Would I go there? Would we?

'I've been to Provence,' I said, taking his hand. 'One

summer when I was a student. To earn money.' It was a summer of sleeping bags and hostels, a time spent living on bread rolls, enormous juicy tomatoes and cheap wine, hours of apple-picking in the heat.

'Not with me,' Patrick said then. 'Really. I've thought about us going to Africa.'

I smiled. It pleased me to know that he had been making plans for us. The gallery was filling up with people, straining past each other to see the paintings. 'Let's sit in the sun for a while,' I said.

We walked downstairs and out the front door to the small garden at one side of the main steps. There were pigeons everywhere, looking for crumbs under seats which were all taken. We spread our jackets on the grass and sat down.

'See what you've started?' he said, taking the food from his bag.

'Why Africa now?' I asked. 'You said you didn't want to go back?'

'Because it felt impossible for all sorts of reasons, I pushed it so far down in myself that it was bearable not to go. Ever since I got the idea of us going together, I haven't been able to stop thinking about it. The small beaches we used to visit along the coast, the size of the seashells. It's all coming back to me. When my father died, my mother found a small apartment. It was easier to keep. The house was sold and somebody else lives there now, but we could drive past.' He sighed deeply and looked at me.

Even though he was just airing the idea, the prospect was exciting and already felt imminent. I had been vaguely planning a trip to Dingle at the end of June, then six weeks away. 'When are you thinking of making the journey?'

'I don't know. December, perhaps.' He shrugged. 'Will you come with me?'

So much of his life was lived before we met, I felt unsure about my place in it. 'You could take Kate?' I suggested.

He shook his head. 'Kate would have no interest in going away in December but winter is the best time and it gets too hot in January. I could speak to my mother and ask if she would spend Christmas there, instead of coming to London.'

Over the next few weeks we spent more time together. I stayed at his home on weekends when Kate wasn't there. When she was with him, we met occasionally on the Heath when the weather was fine. We'd look for cushioning grass around trees which were wide and sheltering, and off the beaten track. On days when he was free, we would spend the whole day strolling through the wilderness or stretched on a hillside in the sun. But more often he came to my room, and once or twice he arrived late at night and without warning.

He promised to invite me on a weekend when Kate was staying but it came to nothing and I became troubled by his silence on the matter.

EIGHTEEN

'It's too soon,' Patrick insisted.

We were on the boat for an afternoon sail. It was late June. The wind had dropped. Grey clouds massed overhead. The weather was warm and sultry. I sat to one side holding the jib sheet, trying to understand his resistance.

'Too soon to tell her about the trip?' I asked. 'She may want to come with you.'

He looked at me unperturbed. 'Why cause a fuss now by raising it?' He watched the sails closely, as he pulled in the main sheet and adjusted the tiller to catch more wind. He was attending to sounds that he loved. Sounds that were new to me, like the creek of timbers high up and the quiet furrow of water made by the keel.

Gulls wheeled over the sea and dropped suddenly from the air. I watched one dive and rise again, a fish hanging from its beak. The boat inched forward. When it gusted, the sails filled and the boom swung out. I had difficulty pulling the sheet in to tighten the angle. Once or twice the boat headed straight into the wind, the sails flapping wildly. I loved it when the wind was steady and the boat found an easy tack, skimming the waves and driving forward at a dizzying pace.

The thought that our trip was a forbidden topic was beginning to hurt. And I felt anxious about Kate. Planning something that was bound to affect her, without her knowledge, felt like a betrayal.

'We already spend most weekends together and you're talking about living with me,' I said.

He had raised the question as to what I would do when Sue needed the room after the baby was born and had suggested that I think about moving in with him.

The boat rolled on the back of a wave. White spray lashed across our faces. He found direction again and tied off the main sail. For a long while he was absorbed in sailing the boat and seemed to forget the bother over Kate. Though still a long way out, we were heading back for land. He kept an eye on our tack and from time to time moved back and forth under the boom. I cleated the jib and sat on the deck of the boat, my back to the wooden ribbing. The centre-mast was polished and grained, thick and tall as a tree trunk. I wondered about the tree it was cut from, a tall pine perhaps or an oak, and how the grain was lovingly planed, and considered the new life the tree was given, to stand and have branches again, not of leaf this time but of cloth.

I suddenly felt homesick. I thought of hedgerows and bohereens thick with fuchsia and meadowsweet. A different sea.

'I was thinking of going back for a week. Home,' I ventured at last.

Patrick leaned back, pulling the boom tight in. The boat moved at speed. 'Some unfinished business you want to tidy up?'

'For heaven's sake!'

'Your home is here now,' he said matter-of-factly.

He shifted the boom to the far side. The boat turned slowly in the water and the bow inched landward. His face was unshaven and the dark stubble gave him a severe appearance.

'How can we live together, if Kate isn't in the picture?'

The sails filled and he leaned back again, all his weight on the sheet. He remained silent and his face was so impassive I began to wonder if he'd heard what I'd said.

'Anyway, I haven't seen my mother since Christmas,' I said.

His face darkened. 'It wasn't your mother I was thinking of. Why don't you invite her over?'

Patrick was paying me back for challenging him over Kate. He made it sound as though I wanted to exclude him.

'Sue's thinking of coming home with me to see her family.'

'I thought we might go together sometime,' he said sulkily.

'I need to check the lie of the land first,' I answered.

'Meaning?'

It dawned on me that Patrick could only see my going without him as a reproach. I wanted to prepare my mother for the fact that I might not be home at Christmas, and that I was planning to move house again.

'See that everyone is well, catch up with things that have been happening at home, put them in the picture about you, give them time to get used to the idea. You're years older, you know.' I didn't like the way the conversation was going and couldn't hide my irritation.

'Isn't it a bit late to be getting worried about that?' It was a sore point and he was clearly stung.

'I'm not worried about it, but I can't pretend I'm ready to settle down.' The words tumbled out. There was a life beyond Patrick that I was unwilling to relinquish, after all. I needed to go back home to revisit the place and to see my mother, but also to find out who I'd become since I left her the September before. I was as unwilling to forfeit my roots as I was eager to fully explore my new freedom.

'You want to have it both ways,' he said after a long pause.

The wind had dropped and we seemed to be at a standstill on our slow, homeward tack.

'Look who's talking!' I snapped. 'Why not discuss plans with Kate now? We can put off living together for a while. I'm not in any hurry.'

'Kate is my responsibility, not yours,' he muttered sullenly.

For the rest of the journey he busied himself and gave me instructions in a curt and precise tone. We came ashore with the tide in the late afternoon and I was relieved to be off the boat. He drove us back to London in moody silence.

When we reached his house it was all in darkness and he persuaded me to stay the night.

'Let's call it a day?' he appealed, referring to the argument on the boat.

Later when we made love, there was a harshness and ferocity as he pinned my wrists together above my head and our bodies wrestled and he thrust inside. I pressed my teeth into the flesh of his shoulder.

'I'm sorry,' he said later. 'I don't know what got into me.'

We lay in the dark under the weight of the blue quilt. Tears stung my eyes. I was tired of fighting, and frustrated by his silences.

'I'm not one of your authors or a character in a story subject to your editorial control,' I said. 'I have a mind of my own. We don't always have to agree on things.'

'I thought what we wanted was the same,' he replied flatly.

The first drops of rain hit the windowpane, and I pulled

the covers round me and turned away from him. He placed an appeasing hand on my waist and, when I didn't respond, he got out of bed, murmuring that he was unable to sleep. He switched on the hall light. His steps were heavy on the stairs.

I tossed and turned, and then heard him coming upstairs again. I didn't stir. He nestled against me, cupping his body against mine and fell soundly asleep. I lay for a long while before I slipped from the bed and went downstairs. I poured a glass of water from the bottle in the fridge and added ice from the tray in the freezer. I noticed a photograph of a woman, pulled forward by a golden retriever, Patrick at her side placing a kiss on her cheek. It was a small photograph, pinned up amid postcards and other photos I'd seen before. It looked like it had been taken with a disposable camera. The colour quality was poor and the overall effect flat, despite the obvious energy of the moment. Handwriting along the border read, 'To Mum and Dad, Richmond '98'.

Gilly lived somewhere near the river. I had once taken the overland train all the way across, and met Patrick there and walked along the embankment, and we had driven back together.

NINETEEN

Sue knocked on my bedroom door early one Saturday to ask if I would like to have breakfast. She was planning an expedition to Kew and invited me to go along with her.

'If you hurry, we could catch the train at eleven,' she called, 'from Islington. James is bringing a picnic.'

I had seen very little of James since he left Dingle to go to boarding school. He was eighteen months older and, then, physically stronger than Denis, winning so many cups at gymkhana his classmates had christened him Pegasus.

He once gave me a prized red rosette because he knew that my mother didn't allow me to enter jumping competitions. Unlike the other boys he wasn't afraid to be seen talking to a girl. I had liked him. So when Sue proposed the trip, I was curious to meet him again.

As the train wound its way across north London, there were glimpses of back gardens, of flowering orange blossom that reminded me of my mother, and climbing frames and swings, of dilapidated sheds with rusty corrugated roofs covered in brambles, of builders on scaffolding, and deep red roses. In the seat opposite two black boys squabbled and bickered over a broken toy.

Sue looked at me and patted her tummy. 'I hope it's a girl,' she said under her breath.

'Girls are angels, as we both know,' I laughed.

We left the train at Kew and walked into the sunshine and through the entrance gate. Sue dug her hands into the pockets of her short leather jacket as we strode through the park and her blond hair reflected the brightness of the sun. I saw young men here and there and looked at them with interest, knowing that James might be one of them. Inside the tropical house, the heat and damp enveloped us. I took off my denim jacket and moved along the edge of the pond, where the water lilies were in bud.

'It's this temperature all the time here,' Sue said, putting her hand on the curve of her abdomen. She stretched her arms and yawned. 'How is Patrick?'

I told her about the plan for South Africa and how I wanted to see Kate again.

'Maybe he needs time?' Sue commented absently, looking at her watch. 'James said he'd meet us here just after half-past.'

There was no sign of him. We rested against the wall of the pond and waited. Gigantic leaves and creamy white lilies floated on the surface of the water like bone china teacups.

A young man smiled as he approached us.

'Do you remember James?' Sue said, giving him a hug.

I thought of the last time I'd seen him at prize day in school, striding bashfully down from the podium with a plaque in his hands, his red school tie perfectly knotted and his shiny brown hair parted to one side.

He was thinner and slighter than his brother now, his hair

in a crew cut, and his look intense.

'The one who got away?' His face creased into a wiry grin.

I took him to mean my leaving Denis as well as home.

'Me or you?' I met his dark brown eyes.

'The pair of us, then. Sue here is responsible for providing a safe house.' He indicated the green backpack slung neatly between his shoulders and looked from me to her. 'Will we make tracks?'

'I thought it was the other way around,' Sue said. 'You were here for years before me.' She began to stroll towards the door and we followed.

'That I was. But it took Sam and yourself to make me settle down.' He opened one side of the white double doors that led out into the park and followed us at a slower pace. I noticed that he limped slightly. It was a relief to breathe cool air again.

'James moved in with us for a couple of months when we arrived first,' Sue explained, slowing her pace to let him catch up.

He walked along beside me. 'I was working on the buildings at the time. There was a band of us ... carpenters and labourers ... working on the Tate Modern. Never forget that. I used to work with a crew then, twenty or thirty of us on the one job. A far cry from fishing for mackerel. I'm on my own now.'

I remembered that the boys worked the summers with their father on the boat. Once he went on to college, James was never around. The family business was left entirely to Denis. I wondered if James minded.

'Would you like to go back and live there?' I asked.

'I've so much work built up here I can't keep up with it,' he answered. 'It would be very hard to turn my back on it. Denis was always the one to stay at home. He got along better.'

We came to a crossroads and Sue led us down a sunny path which opened onto thickets of trees and another pond rimmed with exotic flowers.

'Guess who's sleeping in your old room?' Sue threw over her shoulder.

'You'll need a place to stay once the baby comes? I'll keep an eye out for a good one,' he offered.

Sue looked at me knowingly and back at her brother. 'Eve has plans of her own.'

She waited for me to speak. I didn't want to tell him about Patrick, as if the knowledge would in some way hurt him, which was ridiculous.

'That would be great,' I said hurriedly. 'No other firm plans. Where do you live?'

'Camden. Not too far from Sue's.'

We stopped at a bench beside the pond and put our things down. A tall, livid green, swamp cypress was rooted at the edge of the water and rose into a blue sky.

'Here's fine,' I said, moving towards a sunny hollow in the grass beyond the edge of the shade.

'We brought some food too.' Sue took the rug she'd folded over the basket we packed and spread it on the grass.

'We'll celebrate,' James said, opening his bag and handing me three glasses and a bottle of champagne he had wrapped in ice. 'Do nothing by halves,' he smiled. 'That's my motto anyway.' When he smiled the lines round his eyes made him look older than his years.

He extended two plates wrapped in foil for me to unwrap and uncorked the champagne with a great pop by aiming for the top of the tree. Sue arranged plates and cutlery and we stretched along the edge of the rug as James handed round the brimming glasses. The water in the pond was clear, its surface scuffed here and there by the breeze or the movement of a water bird.

'Sláinte.' He raised his glass. 'A belated welcome to

London. You'll have to meet the gang some Friday night. Remember Digger Foley, he was a few classes ahead of us, and Annie Mulcahy, a sister of Mary's?'

I tasted the chilled bubbly wine for the first time. It fizzed around my mouth. 'They're here?'

'There's a cycling club on Sunday mornings and a lot of them met up that way,' Sue said, propping herself comfortably on her elbow.

'Digger Foley cycles these days?' I laughed at the thought of it. The same Digger was already driving himself to school at seventeen. Somehow pushing himself uphill on a bicycle didn't seem his style.

'He goes to the parties anyway. He's got a computer firm of his own.' James idly cast a small stone out into the water and we watched the ripples widening.

'Computers? He used to run a garage from the shed at home. Maybe there's two Digger Foleys?'

'He's a wizard when it comes to figuring out how things work. It started with cars right enough. He's self-taught.' James searched for another pebble. 'Whatever happened to that pony of yours? The shy black one.'

'Dusty?' I rolled onto my stomach, watching the arc made by James's arm as the stone was launched high into the air over the pond.

'If the park ranger catches you!' Sue scolded, as she passed us each a roasted chicken leg and a napkin. 'Here, eat this instead.'

'I got too tall for Dusty and sold her to the riding school,' I said. 'You wouldn't have seen Clipper. He's a bit nervous and hates cars but he has a lovely temperament. Young Packy Conway mucks out and rides him most days now,' I said, biting into the chicken. 'Can't wait to get back on him when I go home.'

'When are you thinking of going?' Sue asked, the palms of her hands spread over her stomach and her back held straight.

'Next month, if it's all right with Adele. Just for a week.' I looked at her. 'Have you thought any more about coming with me? Your mum would be thrilled.'

'Maybe I will,' she answered. 'It's been such a long time since I've been back home. Not sure if Sam would let me fly at seven and a half months though.'

James finished the chicken and lay back, looking up at the sky, his head pillowed on his hands. 'It's fourteen years since I've been on the back of a horse,' he said dreamily.

He was talking about the accident, the time he was thrown from his horse into the ditch and suffered concussion. He returned to school a hero days later on crutches and a plaster cast on his leg, with an injury that caused trouble for years.

'You still miss it?' I asked, and he turned and looked at me, his eyes clear and bright.

'Of course I do. Hearing you talk makes me wonder if I could take it up again.'

'Give it a try,' Sue said. 'Why don't you and Eve book a ride at a stables one afternoon?' A blue-winged butterfly fluttered in the space between the three of us.

'I'd really like that,' I said. 'Maybe I'd even stop pining for Clipper.'

'I know I could,' James said, thinking it through as the butterfly settled on the grass. 'It's a matter of whether I could bear to just potter around.'

'Do nothing by halves?' I smiled, admiring the ornately patterned white and blue wings.

'It meant the world to me when I was a youngster,' he said. The butterfly lifted again and lighted further away on a reed by the water.

'Let's do it for my sake, if not for yours,' I coaxed.

'Listen to the two of you,' Sue said, gathering the chicken bones and placing them back in the foil. She filled our glasses with what was left of the champagne.

'What do you work at?' James asked, chewing a piece of bread.

'Books,' I said, smiling at Sue.

'What do you do with books?' he persisted.

'I work for a publishing house. At the moment I'm reading stories for the teenage market, as well as copy-editing.' Once the word went round the agents that we were developing a teenage list, we were inundated with stories. My job is to weed out non-runners,' I explained.

'And what do you know about teenagers?' he teased.

'She was one,' Sue intervened, 'and hasn't forgotten what it was like.'

'Thanks,' I said to Sue. 'He's right in a way. What do I know?'

'She was a terrible know-all at school,' James confided to Sue. 'Made it eternally difficult for the likes of me.'

'I love that word *eternal*.' Sue smiled as she packed the cutlery and foil in the basket. 'Especially since you haven't seen each other for a lifetime,' she added, but James took no notice of her logic.

'Denis made up for me.' He glanced at me quickly. 'I kept hearing about you.'

'And I kept hearing about you too. How is Denis getting on?' I gathered the glasses and wrapped each one.

'He's getting married at the end of summer,' he said guardedly, 'to a girl from Boston. She came to Ballyferriter for the summer to learn Irish.'

'Doesn't let the grass grow.' I smiled, thinking of the last time I'd seen him, driving away in the new Land Rover and taking all the energy on the street with him. 'I wanted him to come to London.'

'You didn't know what you were asking,' James said.

Sue agreed. 'Leaving Ireland would break his heart.'

'You understand him better than I did.' I looked from

Sue to James.

'I was an outsider from the beginning in ways that are hard to explain, that's why I'm here,' James added.

I stood up and stretched, taking in the Palm House on the far side of the park and the square of water at the front of it, the wonderful vista through the trees on our right, and I knew what he meant.

TWENTY

'Come back with me?' Patrick asked urgently at a lunchtime reception for one of my titles.

'Where?' It was a struggle to resist.

'My place.'

It would have been easy to say yes. 'Go away,' I said quietly.

He was silent for a second.

'The boat. Friday night. We could have the whole evening?'

I remained stubborn.

'The work's done and nobody's going to miss us. What about sitting over lunch for an hour or two? Then I'll take you home.' He was leaning against the wall with an outstretched hand. Small drops of perspiration under my arms ran inside the raw linen of my shift. He waited for me to answer. My silence irked him. I took the glass from his hand.

'Just lunch?' he insisted.

I sipped the hot smooth taste of malt. He smiled and the colour rose to his cheeks. The glass was warm in my hand and I handed it back to him.

'I'd really like to but unless you've spoken . . . '

'What difference does it make whether Kate knows about us or not, or Gilly for that matter? They don't tell me who they spend their time with.'

The room was beginning to empty. Two waiters collected glasses. It would have been easy to capitulate, to give in and accept the terms, to stretch out on his bed. But I decided Kate was worth fighting for and one day he would see that I was right.

'I never liked Dutch courage.' I indicated the glass and walked away.

Early that afternoon I took the tube home, bringing with me the proof of a biography I was working on. It was difficult to concentrate, even though I had the house to myself. Each time the phone rang, I jumped to answer it, expecting to hear Patrick's voice at the other end. But he didn't call.

I went over his words, and tried to imagine what it would be like to share his house; not to have my own place. Sam and Sue helped me realise the dream of having my own room and an independent base. I wanted to be able to come and go as I pleased. I had no illusions about marriage or family life and I liked my work, which neatly financed my independence. Lost in a sea of voices in the books I edited, I was preoccupied with the lives of different characters for days at a time. It awoke a thirst for experience and a curiosity about living that gave me the feeling of being on a journey with no known destination. Of course, I wanted to be close to Patrick too.

Over the following days, the pleasure and freedom I discovered in returning to my own room vanished. The days at work went by too slowly and I found it hard to sleep at night. The house had an expectant air about it, of silent waiting.

On Friday morning when I arrived at work, I could hear Carol and Patrick talking in the office. The door was open and Patrick was sitting in my chair, next to her desk.

'Good morning, Miss Bennett,' he called without looking up. 'I hear you're moving house?'

A couple of days before, Carol had invited me to stay for the weekend when I told her about the argument with Patrick. I had brought my things to work in a small travel bag.

'Only for the weekend,' I said to him.

His look was affectionate and vaguely amused, as if he rather liked this game of chase and planned to give me a run for my money.

'Kate has organised for us to visit her friends on Saturday night. That should keep me on my toes.' He stood up and stretched. Close enough to touch.

'Good for Kate,' Carol smiled.

'There are a couple of things to be checked for copyright,' I said to Patrick, indicating the biography. 'We could go through it this morning?' Contact, any contact, would alleviate tension.

'I'm afraid I haven't got my diary with me.' There was no hint of hauteur or irritation in his voice, but his unresponsiveness felt like a dig.

'The biography has to have priority,' Carol said to him softly.

He walked to the door, ignoring her comments.

'I'm sorry, Eve. Things don't always move at the rate we'd both like them to. Enjoy the weekend.' He walked through the open door without looking back.

'My!' Carol raised her eyebrows. 'How many permissions still outstanding?'

'Last time I checked, about half a dozen. Let me see.' I pulled out the file to check the printout of quotes and sources of copyright. The dates for permissions received were already marked, but I needed an updated list.

'This was ten days ago.' I unclipped the list and handed it to Carol.

'When's it due at the printer's?' She clicked her tongue as she read the page.

'Midweek.'

The five hundred and forty-two pages with additional plates for photographs and a family tree sat on the shelf above my desk. Adele was currently doing a final read.

'You've done a fantastic job. Patrick's going to have to move on this, don't you worry.'

I stretched my arms and felt the lines of tension along my back. 'It's a nice feeling to have it finished.'

'We'll drink to that this evening.'

The uncertainty between Patrick and myself set my teeth on edge. I tried to keep the turmoil at bay by concentrating on work. Later at Carol's house, hot tears ran down my face, the first since meeting him, and she silently handed me a Kleenex. We sat talking in the kitchen, a bottle of wine open on the table.

'Maybe Gilly's putting the pressure on. Once things settle down again, he'll come round, you'll see.' Carol looked at her watch where she sat with her legs curled beneath her. It was half past one.

'It's going to be all right?' I stifled a yawn.

'It's going to be fine,' she said sleepily.

I was irritated by her composure. Carol had gradually chosen to befriend me partly because Patrick had encouraged it and because our mutual willingness to acknowledge differences encouraged curiosity and trust, and from time to time we began to confide in each other. Perhaps my current conflict with him presented her with an unexpected dilemma that she preferred for the moment to overlook and she concentrated instead on encouraging me to see his better qualities.

The sense of anger I'd begun to feel the day before softened as she spoke. 'When Pete left, I went to pieces. Patrick took me out for lunch, to the pictures, that kind of thing. We've been friends ever since.'

'And Pete?'

'Hope springs eternal. I bumped into him at the Barbican the other night. At least we're on speaking terms again.' She looked as if she was wiping away a tear. 'We met some old friends who were having a party and ended up together.'

I listened to her quietly.

'We've known each other for twelve years,' she continued. 'I was your age when we first met. Some say that love is shared history.'

'And the history one can't share?' I asked, considering my father's absence, and Patrick's current evasiveness.

She was pale and her eyes winced in the light. She placed her elbows on the table, and sipped from her glass.

'You've known Patrick much longer than me.'

'It doesn't mean that I agree with everything he does. What are you going to do?'

'Sue will need the spare room for the baby and he'd like me to move into his house then. I'm not sure it's a good idea any more.'

'A place of your own would give Kate time to get used to the idea of you and Patrick.'

'And Gilly?'

Carol looked at me and answered in a matter-of-fact way. 'Married to her job. She'll be on the bench in five years' time. And she's a strong Labour supporter. She's on the committee of Shelter. Very busy.' Carol got up then and took my glass and hers and ran them under the warm water at the sink. 'I was thinking of calling it a day,' she said, and I stretched in agreement. 'Have a really good sleep,' she smiled.

I sat up for a while reading the *Guardian* before turning out the lights in the kitchen and hallway, and climbing the stairs to the small bedroom.

When I was home at Christmas, my mother had given me two photographs and I showed them to Carol after breakfast next morning. The first was of Connor and myself with my father, taken when Connor was only two years old.

'It's the only one I've got,' my mother had said, giving it to me the day I left. 'He'd like you to have it.'

'I wish you were in it too,' I answered, taking the photo and putting it inside the book I was reading.

'As photographer, I am in a way.'

I leafed through the album and found one of herself taken round the same time.

'You wouldn't want that,' she protested. 'My hair is a show. Take this one instead.'

She handed me a photo of herself, poised for the camera from her garden chair and smiling, probably at Danny, a glass in her hand.

'I prefer the other one,' I said. 'It's how I remember you.'

'Thanks a lot.' She was offended.

My father was seated with the toddler on his lap and I was standing next to him, my head inclined to his shoulder. I handed the photo to Carol.

'Your mum must have taken it,' she said, looking closely at me aged six, short fair hair and in dungarees.

I stirred the sugar at the bottom of my cup.

She lifted the photo of my mother, whose eyes were veiled as she looked down at someone beside her. 'Such classical features,' she commented. 'The dark hair and fair skin. Do you remember when it was taken?'

'Before my dad left. I remember the outfit.' My mother was wearing a moss green jacket and skirt.

'How did she cope?' Carol asked.

'She planned things,' I said smiling. 'She liked company and cooking. She baked on Saturday mornings, all three of us up to our elbows in flour. She combed blackberry bushes for fruit to make jam, and organised friends to stay at the house, or arranged parties and meals for cousins and grandparents. My grandfather was around a lot for a couple of years after Dad left. Then she met Danny.'

The kitchen door was open on to the garden. Outside the sun was already warm and bees hummed around the flowerbeds. Carol talked of putting ice in the fridge to have cool drinks later on, of taking the deck chairs out of the garden shed. She handed me the shed keys while she tidied away the breakfast things. A light breeze tinkled the chimes that hung over the doorway. The earth around the flowers was dry and cracked and I found a watering can in the dusk of the shed and filled it from the kitchen sink to soak the plants.

The urge to ring Patrick was acute. I wanted to say, like a kid, I give up, game's over, then sink into his arms. Instead, I basked in the sun with Carol, absorbing it with thoughts of his body, until I was light-headed.

TWENTY-ONE

When Patrick rang to ask if I was free the following weekend, I was taken off guard.

'I'm sorry about Friday,' he said, and waited for my reaction.

'What about the permissions?' The biography was due at the printer's the next day.

'I've sent you an updated printout of permissions received,' he said automatically.

'We should ask the printer for extra time?' I was still cross with him.

He ignored the question. 'Kate agrees to meet.' From his abruptness, I sensed his desire to put the issue behind us.

Relief swept over me. 'I'm glad.'

'I have to do the right thing, for both of you. It's not as easy as you think.'

'It's not a matter of choosing between us,' I assured him.

Patrick sighed. 'It is to her.'

'Then we must show her that there are other possibilities.'

Out of loyalty to my mother, I had found it difficult to meet my father when the choice was open to me, and I recognised Kate's dilemma.

'The last ten days have been an age,' he said softly. 'I missed you.'

'Me too,' I replied, feeling my anger draining away.

'I'm sorry about the delay over permissions. In fact, I spoke to Adele about it.'

'She offered me a permanent job,' I said happily.

'She's genuinely impressed with the work, and as you know, Adele is no easy taskmaster.'

I reached the house late and knocked on the door. Patrick opened it, his sleeves rolled up and an apron tied round his waist. He kissed my cheek and called to Kate who was setting cutlery on the table. She didn't acknowledge me when I entered the room.

He had cooked her favourite meal, a vegetarian lasagne flavoured with hints of fresh nutmeg and herbs, and was chatting casually about holidays. It was early July and he spoke of taking her to Umbria a couple of weeks later, to stay with her grandmother.

'Dad's going home again and I'm staying there on my own,' she added happily.

We sat down to eat and Patrick and I made several attempts to draw Kate into the conversation. Her answers were monosyllabic and she ate very little, her chin propped in the palm of her hand.

After the meal I sat in the leather armchair looking at an album of photographs Patrick had placed on my lap. He relaxed on the sofa and Kate was on the floor, leaning against his legs, watching television. He had become more reticent.

'What time is Eve going?' Kate yawned when the film ended. The clock ticked on the mantelpiece. It was after eleven.

Patrick crossed the room to the keyboard and sat down to play ragtime, the notes of 'Fly Me to the Moon' rippling from his fingers like liquid silver.

The colour rose to Kate's cheeks as she turned to me. 'Are you taking the train or is Dad going to drive you? The tube's only a few minutes away.'

Patrick fingered the keys quietly, and then stopped playing. 'Eve's staying overnight. We agreed last weekend, remember?' He got up and stood next to me.

'I don't want her to stay. Why does she have to?' Kate said sulkily, as if she were speaking to herself.

'Eve, let me show you around,' he said, ignoring the outburst and indicating the garden. He made it sound as if I'd never been at his home before, but I followed him anyway.

'It's really important to me that you stay,' he said evenly as we stood on the patio. 'There's a sofa bed. We don't have to sleep together.'

We walked into the darkness and sat against the trunk of the low-spreading apple tree. He turned and looked back at the sitting room and at the lit bathroom window upstairs.

'I thought we could all be together without anyone being excluded. Save it up, for when we're really alone?'

The pallor of the image through the frosted window suggested that Kate had changed into her nightdress. I scuffed my heel into the earth. Her bedroom light went on.

He moved closer to me and cupped my head in his hands.

'Kate's the light of my life and she's an only child. She'll come round, she always does. I'll say goodnight to her and then we'll set up the sofa bed.'

I followed him inside. 'Just show me where everything is and I'll be fine.'

He indicated the sofa in the sitting room and a clothes press, and went upstairs.

I removed the cushions and unfolded the frame and made up the bed. I read for a while by the light of the reading lamp until I grew sleepy. The mattress stretched beneath me in its springy frame. The house was quiet and I lay in the summer heat listening to the clock in the hall strike twelve. The garden was moonlit and I could see the magnolia tree and the closed heads of daisies on the lawn.

I heard Patrick's footsteps on the stairs and my heart began to beat faster, my pulse pounding in my ears.

'Shhh . . . ' he whispered, as he lifted the sheet and slid into the bed beside me.

We lay together, pulling the rug around us.

'Kate's sound as a bell.' He held me against him. 'I heard her talking in her sleep.'

My breathing relaxed and my body eased next to his.

'We'll still have to be very quiet,' he warned, stretching the length of his body. My body was tense and wide awake. The patio door was slightly open and I heard the night sounds in the garden.

It was some time before he rose inside me and gripped my hips. My body encircled him slowly at first and then with a growing rhythm, so that the grinding canter of the bed springs rose to a crescendo and the sound impinged on my consciousness. Willow scurried from upstairs, knocking over something on the landing with a clatter before escaping through the cat-flap in the hall. The first blackbird had woken and her song pierced the darkness. It was a quarter to three. Patrick put an arm round me and drew me close, so that my head lay on his chest.

As I drifted into sleep he was still next to me. I didn't

hear his steps on the stairs when he left to go to his own room.

The Yale lock clicking into place was the sound of the front door closing as I woke. I stretched out and found the bed empty. Beyond the window, a drizzle of petals from the white jasmine on the fence sprinkled the grass like confetti. There were foxgloves and a wild rose coming into blossom. Below the apple tree, a garden table and three heavy wooden chairs stood like an invitation. Sunshine hung in the air in a billowing haze.

I wondered if Kate was still asleep and slipped quietly from the sofa bed and took my clothes upstairs to the bathroom. I showered quickly and dressed in blue jeans and a cotton sweater and went downstairs to fold away the bed. The house was silent. The cat appeared at the patio window and I gave it some milk and began to read again.

The front gate creaked. Through the window I could see Kate sobbing, her face in her hands. Patrick's arm encircled her shoulder. I went upstairs to the bathroom and heard them in the kitchen. Kate was still crying and between sobs she said, 'But you promised . . . I don't want to be here . . . ' I ran the tap noisily, but the voices were still audible.

'Come on,' Patrick was saying. 'Eve's my girlfriend. I was bound to meet someone sooner or later.'

I sat on the edge of the bath and waited, hardly daring to breathe.

'I don't want you to,' Kate said.

'It's not personal to Eve?'

Kate started to cry again, and sobbed through her tears, 'I want to go home to Mum.'

'Shhh . . . ' Patrick comforted her.

Kate's cries quietened and she sighed deeply.

'It doesn't change how I feel about you,' Patrick began.

'You don't care about me, and you don't care about Mum. All you care about is her.'

I heard the sound of the patio door being opened.

'I can't pretend I don't care about Eve. Of course I do, but I never wanted to hurt you,' Patrick said after a pause.

'You can't stop me running away,' she countered, as I went downstairs.

'What are you talking about?' Patrick said crossly, following Kate into the sitting room, where he stood looking out at the lawn. Her face was red and swollen and her golden-red hair was pulled back in an angry tangle.

Patrick gestured to me to follow. He asked Kate to tell him again what happened. She spoke haltingly at first and wiped her eyes. When she heard Patrick going downstairs, she wanted to run away but was afraid of being on the streets in the dark. After Willow scurried from the room, she got up and pulled back the blinds and dressed.

She left the house on tiptoe soon after by the hall door at the back. She was going to walk to the tube at the top of the hill but realised that it was Sunday and far too early. She found a call box and phoned her mother. The answering machine was on, and she asked her mother to come and collect her as soon as possible. She walked around and about for ages before she turned back.

She was sitting on the pavement by the front gate with her arms hugging her knees and her head resting on her elbows, half asleep, when Patrick found her.

My face grew hot with shame at the realisation of how careless we had been to sleep together. Over ten years before, the thought of Danny touching my mother's skin and hair had felt shocking. When the prospect of sharing our world with him arose in my mid-teens, I didn't want to know. Sometimes I heard a ripple of laughter from the kitchen or quiet talk coming from the bedroom late at night, or the creak of bed springs. I loathed it. For months I wouldn't look at him when he spoke to me. I fancied the idea of sticking pins in him when he was sitting over a beer satisfied after a long day's work on the sunroom.

'You must be so tired,' I said softly to Kate. 'You need to sleep now.'

I went upstairs to gather my things, the memory of the night warm in my limbs. When I went downstairs again to take my leave, Kate was on the patio stroking Willow. Patrick put an arm round my shoulder and ran his hand through my hair. A hot tear flashed from my eye. I could feel his heart race.

The doorbell rang and he turned to open it.

Outside stood a soft fair-haired, middle-aged woman, with rosebud lips, dressed in a red woollen sweater and dark skirt, a leather bag slung over her shoulder. She extended a hand to me as she walked into the hall.

'I'm Kate's mother, Gilly. I don't think we've met?'

'I'm Eve,' I replied quietly.

Her green eyes observed me. The warmth in her presence partly derived from her compassion.

'Kate left a message asking me to come,' she said to Patrick.

He indicated the patio door resignedly.

'Is she all right? She sounded tearful and said she'd been up for hours,' she said, looking from me to Patrick and following him into the kitchen. I said nothing.

'Is Patrick running you to the tube?' she asked, noticing the car keys in his hand.

Father and mother looked at each other.

'She's so used to having one of us to herself,' Gilly concluded with a sigh. 'Go ahead with Eve. I'll see to her.'

'I'll drop you home,' he said firmly, coming into the hall and swinging my overnight bag onto his shoulder.

'Bye,' I called to Kate, who was still in the garden, teasing the cat with a string, 'and see you again.' I waved to her and Gilly.

'Shouldn't you stay here?' I asked when we were in the car.

'Kate and Gilly have some talking to do. Better leave them to it. I'm sorry about all this,' he said unhappily.

The car moved off and he drove in silence. Daylight was now sharp and unrelenting, and I flinched at its blinding clarity.

Tears stung my eyes. He reached for my hand and held it on his lap. The car slowed down and he adjusted gears with his right hand as he pulled in to park opposite my place. Blustery sunlight swept along the street, glancing off windows and trees. He removed his sunglasses and his eyes winced from the light as he put them in his shirt pocket.

'I had no idea she was awake when I came down to you. I've never seen her like this before.' He withdrew his hand and covered his face momentarily with his palms. 'Damn,' he muttered under his breath.

'I see now why . . . ' My words trailed uselessly away.

'It's time I went back,' he said.

I opened the door of the car. He left the engine running as we walked to the gate. When we kissed goodbye, he ran his hand through my hair and held me close.

TWENTY-TWO

'Sorry about what happened,' he said the next day, as we walked past a grove of elderflower in the Heath. We came into the open on the side of a hill that sloped down towards a small lake. It was sunny and warm and we sat together in the long grass, our shoulders touching. The aromatic scent drifting down reminded me of vanilla and arrowroot.

'I should have known better,' I said apprehensively, glancing at his face, lined and pale.

His manner was short and reticent and occasionally he looked around cautiously, as if he was worried about being seen.

'It's all right if we can't see each other for the moment,' I said, thinking aloud.

He frowned. 'What are you talking about?'

'Kate needs time alone with you.'

'I have thought about that. Believe me, I've had nothing

but time to think in the last couple of weeks.' He was adamant.

Kate had come to stay the previous weekend. He had been worried to hear from her that it was usually nine by the time her mother got home from work. He mentioned it to Gilly on the phone, who said that nobody left the office before seven these days, because of the traffic, and she sometimes stopped off for a drink with a colleague or for a snack before supper. Since the housekeeper was at home with Kate, why did it matter?

'She's not there most of the time,' Patrick said. 'Maybe it explains why Kate is so possessive of me. Things are going to have to change. I think she knows she's being unfair, but can't help herself.'

'It's because I'm not her mother,' I answered.

We were lying back on our elbows and I eased my arms down and lay on my back. He shifted his weight and lay next to me. Our bodies were against each other warming in the sun.

What had happened after I left? When I asked him about it, he was vague.

'She calmed down after a while.'

'Were you angry with her? With me?'

'I was angry at myself.'

My hand ran over a tuft of grass. 'What are you going to do?' I asked quietly.

'What are *we* going to do?' Patrick corrected me.

'Kate says things in the heat of the moment she doesn't mean.' He turned over and lay on his stomach.

'Why do you think it's so hard for her to see you with somebody?' I knew the answer, but did Patrick?

'She sees me as hers. That four-letter word so important to infants, *mine*.'

'She's no longer an infant.'

'Didn't you hate it when your mother replaced your father?'

'Danny was around a lot, before he and my mother became close. Initially my brother and I used to think up names for him, every curse word you could think of. We made no secret of it. But I grew to admire him. He was this great hulking wordless man, who drew designs and saw them take shape and loved working with wood. He was thrown into the deep end and didn't know what to make of Connor and myself. But he won us over. He gave me driving lessons in the station wagon once I turned seventeen and sometimes let me drive when he was going out to see sites and measure up.'

'Maybe Kate will get used to seeing you with me in the same way?' Patrick's brow furrowed. 'I'll spend lots of time with her in the next few months, but want you to be part of it too.'

'We'll see,' I said, thinking that I would make myself a bit scarcer for a while, until Kate got used to the idea.

Her shock and confusion left me obsessively pondering the situation after that. On one level I was strangely buoyant to be the one for whom he placed so much at risk. Never again could I accuse him of hiding his world from me, or of walking away without explanation, as he might have done. Whatever misgivings I'd had about his loyalty to me were banished.

I'd asked Adele about the possibility of taking some time off. We looked at the schedule together and she suggested a suitable week here and there. It was a very busy time because the autumn list was in production and things would not calm down again until mid-September. Staff took it in turns to take a couple of weeks, staggering breaks to the end of August so that things in the office were kept running to speed. Carol had taken some time at the beginning of May and I covered her calls, and she offered to keep things ticking over for me for a week in July.

'Excited?' she asked. 'I've never been to Ireland. Must go one day.'

I couldn't imagine it somehow and it had nothing to do with her views on Cromwell. Carol liked hot weather.

'It's changing fast,' I said. 'Don't leave it too long.'

'I hear Dublin's the place to go to these days?'

'I'll not see Dublin,' I answered.

'I'll keep an eye on Patrick for you.'

'Thanks a lot. Kate's the one who needs looking after.'

'So I hear,' she said pensively. 'She rang me in a state the other day.'

'She did?' I bit my lip, and flinched at her knowing the details.

Carol nodded ruefully. 'She's my goddaughter, you know. We've always got on well.'

She looked at the books on the shelf above her desk and selected one. 'Have you come across this?' she said, changing the subject and handing me a collection of interviews with writers.

I was grateful for her discretion just then, for her attempt to understand rather than judge, and for such a palpable token of her friendship.

'Thanks, I'll borrow it for the week.' I was glad too of the prospect of reading something just for pleasure.

She smiled. 'I found it really absorbing. Let me know what you think.'

The Friday night before I was to leave for Ireland, Patrick suggested he would call round. Kate was staying for the weekend again, and had invited a friend to stay with her. My holdall was packed and lay unzipped by the hall door for the inclusion of last minute things. The kitchen was filled with the sound of laughter and the clink of dishes. Sam and Sue were entertaining friends and from my room I listened for the sound of the door bell as I went down my list and packed a camera into my shoulder bag, along with the air ticket and presents I had bought for my mother and Connor.

Downstairs I could hear the guests leaving and when the door finally closed on the last one, Sue looked in on me. She was seven and a half months now. I said goodbye to her, because she would be leaving early for work next morning, and she gave me a gift for Denis. I told her that Patrick had promised to call, and went downstairs. I waited a while in the scented night air of the garden before going to my room to undress.

It was an hour later when I heard a step on the stairs and the catch of my bedroom door opening and closing. He sat on the bed and placed a hand on the quilt. I turned and found his jacket, which smelt vaguely of yarn and tobacco, cool against my face. The clock ticked on the small table next to the bed as he quietly unlaced his shoes, undressed and lay down close to me.

The impending journey already amounted to a silence between us. The thought that I was going to be a country away from him and that he would be entirely beyond physical reach had registered itself under my skin.

The blinds were open and a shaft of moonlight shone across the floor. We talked quietly of the days ahead and I promised that if, as my mother would say, I was spared and returned safely, he would come with me the next time. The angle of moonlight grew more acute as the night wore on, before it disappeared altogether and darkness reclaimed the room. The birds were up when he moved away from me to find his clothes, and once dressed, he lifted his shoes from beside the bed and tiptoed across the floor. I moved into the warm space he had created and resigned myself to a sleepless night.

I was wakened later by the din of the alarm clock and as

I reached out to switch it off I found a small, blue, gift-wrapped box on the table next to it. I sat up against the pillows and opened it. It was a handmade silver and gold bracelet, and the soft heavy chain felt like treasure in the palm of my hand.

TWENTY-THREE

Boarding the plane, I realised that accents were almost all local apart from a few tourists. Once we were in the air I watched the rainy sprawl of London grow smaller until it vanished beneath the clouds.

The descent to land was made through mist drifting in grey wisps like a benediction, which gave way to a chequered patchwork of fields, spreading beneath the huge wing. The sound of the landing gear being lowered was soon followed by contact on tarmac as the plane tore onto the runway at Farranfore with an ear-splitting roar as the engines were thrown into reverse.

The small arrivals lounge was packed and I saw my mother before she saw me and weaved my way towards her.

When I finally eased free of the crowd, I noticed the walking stick that rested against her waist. She extended her arms and I hugged her close.

'You've lost weight,' she said, holding me from her.

'And your hair?'

My hair was newly trimmed to the top of the shoulder. 'Is it all right?'

'She's made a job of you,' she said so positively that it suggested that the job had been badly needed. 'If I knew you were having it cut, I would've asked you to keep a strand.'

'Mum!' My mother was a constant and reliable presence in my life and up to now there was no need for sentimental gestures. In the past she was rarely given to the kind of volatility that made such tokens of affection necessary.

She smiled and indicated her bandaged left foot. We turned for the door and she walked with the help of the stick as I trailed my bag on its wheels.

'Why didn't you tell me?' I asked, taking her arm and shocked to find that she walked with difficulty.

'It only happened the day before yesterday. I twisted my ankle. It swelled so much I couldn't put my shoe on. It'll take a few days.'

We went through the automatic doors and the cool green air of summer filled my lungs. The ground was wet after rain and the sky began to clear.

'Mary Lynch offered to drive me, but I can just about manage in the car.' She leaned on my arm. The chrome on the blue station wagon was beginning to rust.

'The salt air,' she said resignedly. 'It's doing well given its years.'

I sat in the car and my head rested against the headrest warmed by the sun. On both sides of the road the ditches were high and thick with meadowsweet and brambles. We drove along the main road towards Castlemaine.

'We're in no hurry,' my mother said. 'We can drive straight to the house or stop for a swim, if you like. I brought an old pair of your togs.'

The idea of swimming hadn't occurred to me. It was

typical of my mother to have such a good solution for travel lag.

Her face relaxed as she swung the steering wheel to turn at the bridge. The long, inky blue inlet stretched before us, mirroring white clouds. We left Castlemaine behind. The road followed the water's edge and I watched the wind rippling patterns on the surface and wound down the window to be hit by a blast of salt air.

'How have you been?' I scanned her face for small changes.

'I missed you,' she said. 'I didn't expect to miss you so much, but I did.'

'Enough to come and visit?'

'If I could see where you lived, I think it would help.' She smiled.

'There are so many places to show you.'

'You know, I've never been to London. Apart from the time your father and I went to Vancouver, when you were a baby, and we had to stop-over.' The early years of their marriage in Canada were often recounted.

'You must come and stay.'

She waited for me to say more.

In the distance I could see houses along the cliff that overlooked the strand at Inch, and the glint of sun on a windowpane.

'Is that all you're going to tell me?' she said.

The station wagon slowed down and she found a space in the small car park. Some cars were parked on the sand along the beach, and the tide was out. White rollers broke on the shore.

'I brought a couple of the books I edited, just to give you an idea of the work.'

She took a knapsack from the boot, and her walking stick, and caught my arm with her other hand. We walked along the shore feeling the crunch of shells beneath our feet.

When I slipped into the water, it felt icy. My mother had taken off her bandage and was already out of her depth and swimming parallel to the shore. Soon I no longer felt the cold and swam to where she was floating and steadied myself next to her. For seconds we were lifted and carried on the swell. Then, buffed by a wave, we turned over to tread water.

'Wasn't this a good idea?'

'Love it,' I said. 'A couple of hours ago I was sitting on the tube.'

'You miss the sea in London?' She looked at me.

I smiled happily, but didn't tell her then that the last time I swam in the sea was a couple of weeks before, with Patrick, off the boat at Rye. We were having a row and he dived in, moving expertly through the water, swimming purely for the exercise. I lost sight of him in the waves and was anxious until I saw him double back.

My mother was waist deep and wading towards the shore. From behind, waves knocked and splashed over our shoulders and rolled on. We walked to our small heap of clothes, and the ocean was a din. She threw a white bath towel round my shoulders and dried herself with a green one.

We dressed quickly. My skin was pink and raw all over. Sand blew against our eyes. When we got to the car, she poured two cups of hot coffee from a small steel flask. The aroma drifted towards me as I reached into my leather shoulder bag and took out a group photograph, which included Patrick, taken at a recent launch.

'I'm so glad you have a whole week,' she said, scanning the snapshot as I named my colleagues.

'Who is he like?' she asked, when it came to Patrick, as if he were a long lost cousin. 'He reminds me of someone.'

I looked again at the photo, but couldn't think of anyone just then. 'Maybe the parent of a child at school?' I suggested.

Her skin was paler now from the cold and she looked suddenly defenceless. We were both tired, and she drove in silence until we reached Dingle. We parked by the harbour and went to collect some groceries she'd ordered earlier in the day. An old boat, wrecked years before, was there resting on its keel on a grassy slope. The fishing boats were out, and a few people were forming a queue for one of the passenger boats, which offered trips round the bay to see the friendly dolphin, which surfaced every day in the water.

When I got home, I took my bag upstairs to my old room. There were wild flowers in a vase and a box of tissues and a fresh towel on the bed, but the room looked unlived-in and smaller than I remembered. I found myself inspecting it like a guest. From the landing window I could see across the garden and over the wall to where Clipper grazed contentedly in the field, his copper tail swishing in the breeze. I took an apple from the bowl in the kitchen and went to see him.

'Packy Conway is very fond of him. I told him he could ride him for free if he mucked out on Saturdays and gave him a bucket of oats in the evening. He takes him out most days,' my mother said, when she saw me heading for the field.

Clipper nuzzled my chest and whinnied. He wanted a ride.

'Tomorrow, Clip. You won't believe how out-of-shape I am.'

When I got back to the house Bonnie was barking. It was Danny, who arrived in an old red van.

The following morning I sat in the sunny living room after breakfast. A bee hummed along the glass of the open door. My mother listened while I related the story of meeting Patrick and she enquired about Sue and Sam's house, the office, my world in London.

'He wants us to live together,' I told her.

She'd made raspberry jam and the scent filled the kitchen. She ladled the fruit into jars and gave me the job of making labels.

'And?' she asked, preoccupied with her work, the ladle in her hand.

I took a teaspoon and tasted the crushed sweet berries, irritated by her detachment.

'There's nothing else.' I was irritated too because I didn't know what I wanted.

'What would you like to do?' She stopped and waited for my answer.

'I'm not sure,' I said.

'You're a dark one,' she said, turning back to the jam.

To change the subject I told her about editing the stories for teenagers. Stories were practical in my mother's eyes. They made the world more understandable. They helped to entertain and to send children to sleep, but the fact that someone might want to spend time inventing them or go to great lengths copy-editing them was something she never thought about. There were millions of good stories in the world and she was fascinated that I might be midwife to some fresh masterpiece.

The idea of my living with Patrick bothered her. 'He's older and has seen more of the world. And you're just discovering it,' she said.

Once the jars cooled we would label and lid them with greaseproof paper. I lined them up one by one.

'It's not just that. London's his world, and there's his daughter. I don't want to be taken over.'

She scooped the last of the fruit into a jar and took the saucepan to the sink and returned with a tea towel to cover the jam.

'If I move in, next thing he'll want is a baby.'

'That too?' she asked finally.

'Maybe it's what I want. I don't know. He's got his hands

full with Kate.'

She drew out a chair and sat at the table.

I thought of Patrick and myself, allies in darkness and in light. I was beginning to take his feelings for me for granted. I held out my arm to show her the bracelet, and unclasped it to try on her wrist, which was narrower than mine, rounder and less bony.

'He woos you with gifts,' she said, admiring the silver and gold chain.

'We woo each other. It feels like there's no end to it. He wanted to come with me.'

'Then let him come.'

'I wanted to be at home on my own. It's been too long. You'll meet in London.'

As I spoke the words I imagined my mother and Patrick together. I could see now how it might work. I had worried that he would dismiss her and everyone else here as not worth knowing.

My mother was clearing off the jam spills with a cloth.

'Why don't you invite him over this weekend?' she suggested.

'Curiosity killed the cat,' I smiled at her, and wondered at the idea. Perhaps I could ring him and suggest it, or raise it when he rang.

In that way, my mother and I talked, and made expeditions, and the days ran into each other. Everywhere I went I caught glimpses of people I knew. Mornings were overcast and humid but by lunchtime it was warm and sunny. The windows were left open in the afternoon, and I grew used to the incessant birdsong, the salt on the air, and banks of fuchsia coming into flower along the road. I lay on the front lawn on a carpet of daisies when my head grew too hot in the sun to read. A couple of old friends from school visited in the evenings and sported new cars and new babies. The kitchen table was moved out of doors for meals, and we sat in the setting sun at the front of the house.

Her bare legs had birthmarks along the shin that looked like large freckles, and one ankle was still wrapped in a bandage. She stretched as she yawned. I scanned her face.

'When you met Danny. How did you know you could love him?'

Her eyes rested on me. The distant call of a curlew piped from the shore.

'When I met Danny, he understood me without saying anything. Words would have gotten in the way. He liked that I stood on my own two feet. It didn't threaten him.' Her voice was calm, and bidding me to understand.

'I'm sorry we were so mean to him. You belonged to Connor and to me. I couldn't bear the idea of anyone touching you. It wasn't personal to him.' I was thinking of Kate's distress.

She shrugged. 'Water under the bridge. Danny took the brunt of it.'

The wingbeat of starlings passing over our heads caused me to look up. As evening fell they moved south in small colonies to nest for the night, their flight a kind of spell in the dusk, mysterious and governed by laws invisible to me.

'Danny kept his own place for years. It never bothered me,' she said.

It was almost dark now and we sat in the stillness, listening to the sound of a car on the road, and watching the beam of headlights in the sky.

There was resignation in her voice. 'You've got to make your own mistakes.'

'I wish London wasn't so far away,' I said.

'Me too,' she answered. 'You must think about what to do with Clip, not now but long-term.'

We gathered plates and glasses, and I stacked them to

load the dishwasher.

I came downstairs early on Thursday morning to slip out for a ride with Clip. Danny was already there, whistling softly as he set fresh coffee on a tray to take upstairs.

'Eve, your mother will be fifty this summer and I've been thinking about a present,' he confided.

'Will she?' I asked, my heart sinking at the prospect of not being around.

'I want it to be a surprise,' he said quietly. 'A trip to London before she goes back to school.'

'Danny!' I said happily. 'But you know my mum and surprises?'

'She'll think it's a takeover.' He smiled. 'But we'll do our best to convince her otherwise.'

'Will you come with her?' I asked.

'It might cramp her style,' he said, smiling at me. 'Not this time.'

'She could stay with me,' I offered.

'Or you might like to stay somewhere with her? That's what I wanted to ask you about. Do you think you could find somewhere that she'd really like, a bit out of the ordinary?'

'I'll have a think and let you know,' I said. 'We're talking about late August?'

'You might phone me at the office,' he replied. 'And in the meantime I'll try to sound her out, without giving anything away.'

'Danny. It's a great idea,' I said, giving him a hug.

He lifted the tray to take it upstairs and I went to find my raincoat in the hall.

Packy continued to call each morning to feed and water Clip, even though we'd given him the week off.

'What would you sell him for?' He was standing in the paddock, the cowlick on his forehead brushed back and glistening. He held Clip by the reins.

'He's not for sale,' I said, stung at the thought of parting with the horse. 'Thanks for looking after him for me. You'll be the first to know if I think about selling him.'

'I was just goin' to give him a run to the stream,' he offered.

'He likes that,' I said. 'But I fancied a ride myself this morning.' He'd carried me to the stream for years and dipped his head to the water, so low I had trouble not sliding over his neck. Sometimes I'd stand him in the dripping rainwater under the trees, as gnats thickened in the humid air and he swished his tail at flies on his rump. Now he was eyeing me as I ran the water jet round the yard.

I walked over and rubbed his forehead and the white markings on his face, while Packy put on the halter and saddle for me.

'He's a fond horse,' he said, straining to reach the belly band. 'You must miss him something terrible.'

'Knowing he's well looked after makes it easier and I've found a place to go riding at the weekends. Remember James Corrigan from the pier, he went to London a couple of years ago?'

'I know the house,' Packy said, 'but I've never met him.'

'Well anyway, I met him a few weeks ago and we decided to try it out one Sunday. It's just for an hour and it takes time to get used to a strange horse. Nothing like going out with Clip.'

At the sound of his name the horse's ears pricked up and he shifted his weight, and his brown coat gleamed.

'James is a good horseman?' he enquired amiably.

'It's a bit of a saga, and I'll tell you about it sometime,' I explained. 'There's no one like him, when it comes to that, with the possible exception of yourself.'

Packy raised his eyebrows and blushed at the compliment and secured the stirrup.

Clipper was saddled and ready and he pulled at the bit

impatiently. Packy rubbed his forehead and handed me the reins. Then he gripped his palms to offer me a leg up and I held onto the saddle for balance and eased myself over. Clipper jagged his head up and sidestepped, haunches moving beneath me when I pressed the stirrups. I tightened the reins and guided him to the gate of the yard, and the horse drew forward from my grip, eager for a run in the long paddock.

Patrick phoned while I was out and I rang back only to find the machine on and I left a message. He didn't return my call that evening nor next morning and I rang him at the office that afternoon, but Doris told me he'd left early and would not be back in work until Monday. The weather had changed and the rain beat on the windowpanes and spilled down on the yard and the fields and on the trees. Water dripped from the eaves.

TWENTY-FOUR

At work a neat stack of telephone messages and faxes awaited me. The typescripts I was working on were arranged as I'd left them in a row across the table, with lists of editorial comments and markers. I dialled Patrick's extension but there was no answer.

During the morning the phone on my desk rang several times. An author wondered whether her proofs were ready for correction and if we might meet up at the end of the week. Tony popped in to ask if I had time to look at some ideas for a cover design. It was business as usual. Nobody mentioned Patrick.

It was heading towards eleven and already warm outside when Carol rang. After she hung up, I opened the skylight window in a daze and heard birds singing in the little park across the road. Where could Kate be? I resolved to work through until lunchtime and then drop round to Patrick's house.

He answered the door, half opening it as if he were expecting an intruder. His unshaven face was creased with lines. For seconds we just looked at each other.

'Patrick,' I murmured.

'You'd better come inside,' he said finally.

As the door closed behind us, I wanted to hold him close. He stood tensely, his arms by his side.

'I'm so sorry,' I said, running my hand across the pale blue shirt he was wearing. He'd lost weight.

'It's not your fault,' he said, abruptly sinking his hands in the back pockets of his jeans. 'Who told you?'

'Carol, this morning,' I answered, taking in the afternoon silence of the house, the drawn blinds that kept the sunlight in the garden.

'She's always been fond of Kate. Ever since she was a baby. The police are doing what they can. Gilly and I made statements, and they've talked to all the neighbours and her classmates. I keep hoping she'll walk in that door. When I heard the bell . . .' His voice trailed off.

He threw a black-and-white poster across the table; beneath Kate's face were details of where she was last seen and a number to contact. They'd used a school sports day photo of Kate wearing a white latex T-shirt, her hair in a ponytail, her face turning to look directly at the camera. The clarity of the image and her freckled, questioning face brought home the reality of her disappearance.

'Adele's taken over my work, so I've hardly been in the office.'

'Why didn't you tell me?' Tears sprang to my eyes.

He looked tired. 'The week went by so quickly. I spoke to your mother on Thursday morning and everything was fine with you. I didn't want to ruin your week off. Since Saturday it's been a complete roller coaster. From one hour to the next, I don't know what's happening.' He rubbed his forehead anxiously. 'There's so little one can do.'

'You didn't tell me because you think it's my fault.' It was hard to accept his silence.

'The police are breathing down my neck. They're watching this house right now. The less you have to do with me the better. When it comes to being a father, I've obviously screwed up.' He bit hard on his lip. His unshaven jaw trembled.

'Stop blaming yourself. I don't care about the police. It's not a crime to sleep with you.'

'It might interest you to know that I'm chief suspect, in the event of . . .' He turned and left the room.

I looked at him in alarm and followed him into the kitchen. I placed a hand on his shoulder. Neither of us spoke. He removed my hand and moved away from me.

'For your own sake, the less contact we have the better.' The words penetrated like a sting. Patrick stood with his back to me. The sound of the element grew as the water heated in the kettle.

'You don't want to see me.'

'I didn't say that,' he said contritely, and when I didn't reply, he asked, 'Tea or coffee?'

I wanted nothing, but he placed two cups on the worktop anyway.

'I'd no idea Kate would react in this way. It's crazy,' I said.

'So Kate is crazy now?' Patrick stormed.

'I'm not saying that,' I said quietly. 'When was the last time you saw her?'

He handed me a cup of tea, and took one himself and we went back to the sitting room. He stood against the wall by the radiator, and I sat near him at the table. He told me that she'd arrived early on Saturday, going over each detail mechanically, as if he were recalling the moments before a death. In the afternoon the friend who was due to sleep over changed plans and asked if she could stay instead a couple of weeks later, when she got back from holidays with her parents. In the evening, Patrick tried to talk to Kate about us, telling her he would like to live with me and perhaps marry one day.

'If I'd kept my fucking trap shut . . .' he said angrily.

She hated the idea and had sobbed and pleaded with him. He assured her that he would always be her father, and that our relationship would not change his love for her. He said that her face was a mask and before he finished speaking she had crossed the room and ran upstairs. He could hear her packing her clothes. When he tried to stop her, she pushed past him and went into the bathroom to gather her things. She slung the bag over her shoulder, rushed downstairs and left without a word.

He had caught up with her in the street and tried to reason with her, but she said that she was taking the train to Richmond and pulled her arm free. She began to walk uphill in the direction of the station. He offered to drive her to her mother's but she walked on, and he accompanied her in silence as far as Gospel Oak, where she bought a single ticket to Richmond. She told him not to worry because she had her own key even if her mother wasn't back, and she would ring the following day.

'I let her go,' he said, 'and assumed she was going straight home as she always did. If only I could turn back the clock.'

'She hasn't been seen since the Saturday I went to Dingle?' I asked.

He shook his head, and looked past me into the distance, his eyes glazed.

'That's almost ten days ago.' I began to feel numb.

When Gilly rang on Sunday to say that she would meet Kate at Richmond station as usual, Patrick realised his daughter was missing. He'd gone back to the station. The man in the ticket booth suggested he talk to the police.

'They can check the CCTV. If she got off somewhere else,

they might have it on camera,' Patrick mimicked his polite, officious tone.

Gilly's house was checked. There was little to prove she'd even gone home on Saturday evening, except that her sleeping bag was missing from the top of the linen cupboard.

'The police have been asking all sorts of questions. I feel like a criminal.'

'What do the police think?'

'They've contacted Interpol. Issued photographs to all ports and airports . . . checked with the voluntary agencies in case she's sleeping rough. So far we've held off on media. Gilly can't bear the idea.'

I thought about what Patrick had said about Umbria. 'It would take days to get to Italy overland.'

He nodded. 'I thought of that, too. She has taken all of her pocket money – she had a credit card account. I haven't wanted to upset her grandmother, so I rang Antonia about something else on Wednesday and again on Saturday. I had to be really careful because she asked about Kate.'

The possibility of Kate hidden in the back of a long-distance truck, persuading the driver to allow her to travel in the sleeping cabin as they crossed France or Germany on a fast autoroute, was real enough. Or she might have boarded the Eurostar, if she'd had enough money to buy a ticket. The idea of having a favourite grandmother in Italy gave the idea of running away a frisson of excitement that I decided to spare Patrick just then.

'I went to Rye yesterday.' His eyes shone desperately. 'When I'm at the boat, I feel that she's safe.'

'Any sign that she's been there?'

'Nothing.'

He told me that ever since the alarm was raised he could feel her weight against his chest, the solid weight of her when he held her as a baby. The sensation was so palpable and strong and he was so overcome with dread that he found it hard to attend to anything else. It was why he needed to be alone and why he found it difficult to phone me when I got back from Ireland. Even though it was the tenth day and the police were losing hope, he refused to give up.

I let him talk on. Before Kate was born, he told me, while Gilly carried her to full term he was plagued by dreams of losing a baby. The small infant left by the wayside would turn out to be his own, abandoned by him in a fit of forgetfulness. He would go to the filling station, leave the baby down and drive away without it. Sometimes he woke in a sweat to find Gilly awake too and surprised at his anxiety. When Kate was born, the sense of tenderness and attachment he felt was instantaneous. His anxiety vanished. Now it was as if that dream had returned to haunt him.

His back was to the wall and his head rested against it. His voice was so low I could barely hear it.

'If there's any news, Carol will pass it on to you,' he promised, looking at me guardedly.

I got up and opened my arms to embrace him and we stood together for a moment in the dusk of the room. The smell of sweat and panic from his skin was rancid.

'I want to stay with you,' I said.

'It will end soon,' he said firmly, releasing me from his arms.

We stood awkwardly at a distance. Our eyes met. Outside in the sunshine we could hear the sounds of people going about their lives.

'And then?' I asked, turning to go.

'And then?' He stared at me blankly before managing a weak smile. I was daring to ask if we had a future.

'We'll all live happily ever after?' I said, opening the door to blinding sunshine, and closing it behind me.

TWENTY-FIVE

I stand up from the warm water and pull the stopper chain. Water gurgles noisily from the white cast-iron bath as it drains. Carol's house has an old-world feel and is sparsely furnished. The floorboards in the bathroom are covered by a threadbare rug. I wrap myself in a towel and place the small blue bottles of orange and lavender oil back on the shelf before returning to the guest room. As I dress I catch glimpses of myself in the pockmarked mirror. My face is pale, no longer streaked with mascara and tears, and bears few traces of the anguish of the night before. Only a dull hammering at the back of my head, as if my skull has been tightened with a vice-grip, recalls the fiery taste of Black Bush. I pick up the bottle to take it downstairs.

It's Wednesday and Carol calls from the hall to say she's going round the corner to the bakery for fresh rolls. When I go into the kitchen, the kettle switches itself off and there's a radio news report of a cardboard city which was recently cleared. I put the bottle back in the drinks cupboard of the pine dresser and rinse the coffee-maker. The reporter describes the majority of homeless as Scottish, with some Irish and Welsh.

After a concert at the South Bank with Sue one night in the winter, as we made our way to the Hungerford Bridge by the concrete terrace, we were stopped by a young woman with short red hair, wrapped in an old blanket. Her teeth were discoloured and broken. Ahead of us, the walls were lined with cardboard boxes and people in blankets crouched between the pillars. Several youths whizzed by on skateboards. A cutting wind hurt our eyes and ears. She patted her great stomach, and there was a stench of urine and poverty from her clothes and body. I took a step backwards.

'My first baby, love. Would you ever be so kind as to buy me some milk and bread?' She was Irish.

I didn't want to miss the last train, or lose sight of Sue who was already yards ahead.

'I'll pray for you always . . .' she said to me.

I handed her some coins and walked away along the echoing pavement towards the open area by the river.

'She must be living here.' Sue indicated a huddle of figures in the corner, a bearded man twice her age, his eyes blood-shot, hand cupped over a match flame as he lit a cigarette, dark hair falling over his pale face.

We climbed the steps to cross the bridge. The lights along the river blew in the wind. Beneath us the river was choppy.

When Carol returns from the bakery, she turns down the radio and opens the kitchen door, letting in the sultry summer air. She rummages for the toaster under the worktop and plugs it in, and places some bread inside.

'I'm afraid I hit the bottle last night,' I say, wincing. 'Would you like some coffee?' I pour one for her.

'Thanks.' She sits down. 'Have some toast and marmalade.'

'I'm so confused.'

'The police investigation? Anyone would be.'

'In addition to that, we can't have any contact.'

'He wants to protect you.' She passes the toasted slices across the table. The coffee is smooth and aromatic. 'For your own sake, it's best not to interfere . . .' she insists.

'He told me you were a rock.'

'What are friends for?' Carol asks. 'When he rang first thing on Monday he was beside himself. I got to the house and he just sat there, wordless, tears running down his face. He must have spent the night distraught, pacing the floor and listening for sounds at the door. It didn't help that Gilly was furious with him and his mind was a tangle of conversations with her. When he finally did begin to talk it was hard to make sense of what he was saying. I was really concerned that he was going off the deep end. He'd been to the school and thought he glimpsed her. He was concerned about the need to tell you and couldn't figure out how.'

'I was angry that he didn't.'

'I offered to phone you while I was with him. That way he was at least present.' Carol looks at me with some sympathy.

I begin to wonder how anyone could be cruel enough to cause so much distress, and feel a wave of fury against Kate.

'After eight thirty he waited outside the school gates, saw shoals of girls drift by on their way in. Teenagers in uniform with bags slung over shoulders – they all look a bit the same. He stood scanning faces for a long time and then thought he saw her in the distance. Too far away to tell for sure, but the outline of hair and clothes was hers and he moved towards her. When he was only yards away, she turned and it was someone else altogether. He's clutching at straws. I offered to go myself on Tuesday to save him the anguish.'

Carol sits with one hand cupping her chin, preoccupied

with the situation. Her face is full of care and concern. When the last of the coffee is drunk, I get up to clear away the table.

'What do you think has happened?' It's the question that keeps me awake at night and that I can't really ask and that I don't expect an answer to but it's a relief to speak the words. The turn of events is like a bad omen. If anything happens to Kate, how could we ever see each other again? How could making love be making death? The night the three of us spent together comes back to me. Its darkness and heat.

'She's going to be all right,' Carol says firmly.

'You really think so?' I ask in surprise.

She nods resolutely. 'Any other outcome is unthinkable.' She glances at her watch and picks up the car keys. The office is twenty minutes away.

It is not the time to name fears. The kitchen door is open onto the garden and the sky is now overcast and strangely broody. A breeze blows and the chimes tinkle. It is time to go to work.

That evening in Carol's house I pull back the blinds and sit at the window, the lights of London all around me. When I'd been with Patrick at the top of Primrose Hill in the gathering dark, the city lay glimmering at our feet. Now the night sky is clear and the crescent of houses on the far side of the green shines in the distance and moonlight falls across the floor. I think of Patrick alone in his house maintaining a vigil, of the phone ringing with good news of Kate, or of her suddenly appearing at the door.

Since I arrived in London I have been alone and free. There's little I can do. I love Patrick and nothing that has happened diminishes what I feel, except my right to express it. I long to be with him and to hold him close, but for now I have to get used to keeping that longing to myself.

The silence of this house at night is comforting. I wonder if it sounds so to Carol, quiet in a restful way, and whether she's ever afraid of the dark, like I am, or of sleeping in an empty house on her own. She stays up to hear *Book at Bedtime*, and I realise that I admire her courage and confidence in living out her life on her own, not needing to depend on tags, like mother or wife, but on her own self.

TWENTY-SIX

On the phone Patrick recalls his first sight of Kate standing on the granite steps of the old vicarage in a pale blue summer dress as if in a dream. He tells me that he sees her in a way he's never seen her before. Not since she was handed to him after the long night of her birth has he seen her from such a distance or with such hope. His voice is hoarse. She could be anyone else's daughter, taller than he noticed, red hair tied in a ponytail, legs and arms bare, the smiling, anxious face, the maturing body of a young woman. He knows that her return is temporary, a matter of four or five years if he's lucky. He wants to tell me the whole story.

He embraces this stranger who looks up at him, expectant and familiar, saying, 'Hi Dad!' from behind the veil of her tearful eyes.

'I'm not sure I know her at all,' he confesses. '*You're not mad?*' He imitates her voice. '*I thought you'd be really mad with me. I'm sorry.*' He gasps, 'Imagine, she thought I was going to be angry with her?'

He is so delirious and I'm so stunned that I just listen and catch myself from time to time staring at the receiver. I'm back at Sue's and she and Sam are in bed when the call comes.

He tells me how he stood at a distance watching the leave-taking from the hostel. The small group of youngsters who had befriended her gathered round the shiny black Citroën. I imagine the car now, as they must have, powerful and sinister, sweeping across the gravel to fetch her. I see the laughter and tears, the surprise that she couldn't stay any longer, and how she shrugged and gestured, to explain that her parents had come to take her home. He says they whispered to one another in their own tongue, repeating the word *kuchee* and glancing furtively at him as they bade farewell in turn, here and there a pat on the shoulder, a motherly one taking Kate's face in her hands and rubbing her cheeks. Girls with black hair and dark skin, one with a baby in her arms. Patrick wonders about the homes they left behind, the abandoned houses in rural towns and villages, the brothers and fathers, the mothers and sisters, their happiness despite displacement.

Once Kate was ready and seated in the back beside Gilly, all three of them waved one last time.

'When she finally said goodbye and the car began to move, she cried a lot, but apart from looking a bit pale, she was fine.'

'She's home!'

'She was getting a bit tired of hostel food, I suspect. In retrospect it's obvious, I suppose. She went to Victoria and took a train to Dover, with the idea of going to Italy as we had thought. She was asked to produce a passport at the ferry and couldn't board without one. She was hanging about the harbour area and joined a group of refugees she saw coming off a boat, who were on their way to a hostel on the Kent coast.'

'Just like that?'

'There were some teenagers she sat next to, waiting for a transfer by bus to that hostel. It's all a bit vague really, but she was safe enough. Couldn't have been in better hands.'

'It's incredible, and what a relief.'

There is a pause, and Patrick's voice changes tone.

'You and I have some talking to do. Let's have lunch tomorrow, if you're free?'

The hall is in darkness. The headlights of passing cars momentarily light the stained glass of the windowpane. Tomorrow's list is on my desk at work and I'm not sure what to say.

'We could take a sandwich to the park,' I offer quickly.

'I'll wait for you outside Maisie's, just before one.'

It's too late to wash my hair. What am I wearing to work tomorrow? Will he really notice? Nothing seems to matter now that Kate is home and safe. Who cares about hair? I run upstairs to tell Sue. She raises herself on her elbow. Sam is sleeping.

'Great,' she whispers.

I must let Patrick know of my decision to find a place of my own, and go to my room and undress in a dream. I'm so wide awake it might as well be morning. In the end I fall asleep going over an imaginary conversation and dream of trying to speak to him, but there are lots of people I don't recognise standing between us.

When I see him, he has already been to Maisie's and selected sandwiches and tins of juice. There's a darkness around his eyes, and he has lost more weight. He holds out a hand and I gingerly take it. We walk round the corner to the small park across the road. There are lots of people lying on the grass in small groups, their shoes kicked off, and we walk past them to where the lime tree spreads its branches, and sit in the dappled shade.

'It was so strange waking up today,' he says. 'For the last week, when I did get some sleep, I wanted to die rather than wake up.' He leans back, his hands folded under his head, looking at the sky.

'And what was it like this morning?' I ask, feeling the gap between us, and the warmth of the sun on my limbs.

'As if I'd been freed from prison. I could see Kate's face when she told the policeman she was sorry for all the trouble. Davis, the guy who was breathing down my neck, actually shook my hand, and mentioned his own kids. "Never a dull moment," he said before he left us.'

Patrick is relating this to me as if we'd never been separated. Whatever hiatus existed while Kate was missing is now over. I am still cautious.

'So it's all right for us to meet now?'

'Of course it is.' He laughs.

'So Kate was fine all along? She could have rung home,' I said.

'Once she'd run away, she was frightened to phone home. Afraid of our anger. She had no idea we were so distraught. She promised never to do that again.' He hands me a sandwich and a tin of apple juice. 'She was so sweet,' he continues. 'It seems she'd been thinking about moving in with me for some time, but didn't want to hurt her mother by raising it. When she heard that I wanted to share the house with you, it was the final straw.'

The sun goes behind a cloud and summer air shivers my skin. He sits up, props himself on his elbows and lifts the sunglasses from his eyes.

It hadn't occurred to me that Kate might have wanted to move into her father's house.

'She felt angry that I never asked her to live with me. I should have foreseen that.'

'And Gilly?' I ask, opening the tin of juice and

drinking from it.

'I'm sure she'll miss seeing Kate every day. Anyway, we're talking about the end of summer before school starts and Gilly is taking three weeks off in August. I didn't want to make the final decision without consulting you. I've really missed you.' He sighs, casting the sandwich aside and laying his head on my lap.

Our bodies are touching but I feel so estranged.

'It would be a good idea if you and Kate could work things out, without having to worry about me. I don't want to hurt anyone.' I move away from him. He sits up and reaches out a hand to draw me close. 'Anyway, I have plans of my own.'

Patrick looks at me in surprise. 'What plans? Last week was terrible for all of us. Kate knows that I'm serious about you and maybe it was the only way she could challenge it.'

'She could have *asked* to move in.' I am angry and he sees it. 'Why did she have to run away to make her point?'

'Maybe she did ask, not in so many words, and I was deaf to it.' He changes the subject. 'Did you speak to your mother about us?'

I want to let him know that I've already started looking for a flat, but the words stay in my throat.

'Yep.'

'And?' He is all curiosity and charm.

'And?' I throw the question back at him.

'What does she think?' He wants to humour me.

'Fee, fie, foe, fum, I smell the blood of an English man!' I mimic a pronounced Kerry accent.

'I was born in Cape Town.' He smiles.

'She invited you to stay.'

'She did? When are we going?'

'Single beds. No hanky-panky. Seán, the parish priest, will be round to check you over.'

He looks at me sceptically from where he sits on the grass

and moves closer, running a hand along my spine. 'Then we'll have to make up for that in the meantime.'

My body beneath his hands is numb. Still waiting. The news hasn't really sunk in.

'What if Kate was still missing?' I say, crossing my legs under my dress lotus position.

'I wouldn't want to involve you.' His eyes meet mine.

'I am involved.'

'Not when it comes to taking responsibility for Kate.'

'It's not that simple,' I say stubbornly.

'Be happy with me?' His mood is buoyant. 'Let's celebrate?' He holds up a tin of juice.

'The return of the prodigal?' I say, raising the juice.

'The return of the prodigal.' He smiles.

We clink tins.

'I've told Kate you're moving in as soon as we get back from Italy. Just so that she's used to the idea.'

'Really?' I'm annoyed that he takes it for granted.

'Yes, really.'

'So much has happened. I thought it might be best if I found a temporary place. Carol's also invited me to stay. Sue and Sam need to decorate my room for the baby.'

I wait. He does not respond.

It's time to go. We stand up and he looks at me, and leans over to kiss. Our lips meet hesitantly.

'Let me see you,' he says, taking my face in his hands and then running his hand over my dress to brush off the small blades of grass that cling to the fabric before we return to the office.

TWENTY-SEVEN

Kate throws me a cursory glance from where she's sitting at the other side of the table in the boardroom at the office. She sips a tin of Coke and listens to the music on her earphones. Her father has come in to collect some work from Adele and asked me to drop in and say hello. Kate's hair is cut short to her ear lobes and falls across her face. She looks altogether paler and taller because she's lost weight, and she averts her eyes when I enter the room.

'Hi!' I say, going round the table to meet her. She continues to sit wordless and detached and places one hand over her earphones to indicate that she's listening to her CD. Sounds up and down the building of phones ringing and voices in conversation fill my ears, reassuring me that there's another world to escape to.

'We were all worried about you,' I say.

Kate shrugs, and presses the controls of the CD player in her hands. Her face is absorbed. There's a concentrated look in her eye.

'It's a really lovely brooch,' I try again, admiring the clay disc, in shades of yellow with a dark outline of the sun, on her lapel. She places her hand over it protectively, and rubs the surface.

'Ali gave it to me,' she says quietly.

'Did she make it at the hostel?'

'Make this?' Kate asks scornfully. 'You'd need a kiln to make this.'

'Of course you would. I love the colours.'

'It's just different yellows. What's so great about that?'

'The contrast with the dark outline. It's like the sun.'

Kate says nothing for a moment.

'Yeh,' she agrees finally, and takes off the earphones. 'It is the sun.'

I am relieved when the door opens and Patrick appears. His hair is swept untidily from his forehead. His eyes appeal to me for patience as I leave the room.

'See you end of next week?' he calls after me.

'Sure,' I say. 'Let's speak on the phone before you go.'

Early on Sunday morning I drive out with James to a riding school he discovered beyond Milton Keynes. These trips have become what he refers to as a regular 'date' and he calls to the house before seven.

James phoned on the day after the picnic and our lessons began one morning when the sun was bright and the sky so blue to the horizon that it was easy to believe it was shining everywhere in the world, in Ventry and all across Ireland and over the sea. The cobbled yard of the stables had the familiar smell of horse dung, and a small, energetic woman with cropped silver hair was already tending the horses with oats and water.

I stood looking around at the trees in the distance and the

flowering gorse along the ditches, as she introduced James to each animal – the docile bay and the chestnut, which were good for teaching children to ride, and the lively ones outside, roaming in the small paddock. Because she was a keen rider herself and a regular participant in show-jumping competitions, it was a small school and my hopes about being able to trek for miles across fields came to nothing.

She was drawing James out about his fall, that time all those years ago when his horse failed to clear the ditch. I could see that her understanding of the situation was immediate. She invited us each to choose a horse for ourselves, and James looked at me in consternation. We were standing at the edge of a small fenced paddock and I asked the woman which horse she preferred to ride herself. She walked over to a spirited mare called Molly and stroked her long neck. She was gentle in temperament, the woman said, but needed careful handling.

'There you go,' I said to James decisively. 'That's your ride.'

Already Molly had dipped her head to his hands and he laughed nervously as he gave her some oats from the bucket.

'She has boundless energy,' the woman said to him. 'Just keep the reins short and you'll be fine. Come with me to the tackle room.'

'I'm really happy to just watch. You take her,' James announced suddenly, his face white.

The woman looked at me.

'I'm going to ride the grey,' I said and followed her inside, returning shortly with hats and protective jackets and tackle for both horses to where James was standing in the sunlight.

How we later found ourselves cantering around the small field with ease had something to do with the woman's confidence that it was simply a matter of James mounting the horse and riding her. There were no explanations or theories, only precise instructions and technical know-how thrown in here and there that led to something happening so naturally one could almost feel oneself in the hands of a higher power. Or like responding to a remote control. James quickly began to look more relaxed, and soon he was cantering to a steady rhythm, leaning down every now and then to whisper in the horse's ear. As we drove back to the city that first time he was exhausted and pale but in good spirits.

We've been out occasionally since then and relish the sense of freedom it affords – it's a reprieve from everything else in the week. There is a faint air of teasing in his face when he looks at me and asks a question, as if he already knows the answer. And I find myself going out of my way to say things that will confound him or amuse him, partly to see him relax in a moment of laughter, to see all the tension in his long lean body drain away.

When I start looking for a flat in earnest, I decide to ring him to ask for his help and he promises to phone back later in the week.

In the meantime, I go to see several each evening in small Victorian terraces, which are dingy and smell of age, and are barely affordable. There are single bedrooms at the top of stairs, with net blinds and old damask curtains over grimy windows half-washed by the rain. The kitchens are small with plastic chairs and painted tables. No comparison with Sue and Sam's house.

I am convinced now that a place of my own is the right decision. Carol's house would always be hers and the idea of sleeping there with Patrick would be strange. Sue sometimes accompanies me to look at flats, and says that the walk will do her good. She quickly tires and sits waiting for me on the front steps, in the warm evening sunshine, listening to the rustle of a breeze on a lone palm tree along the terrace. Her baby is due soon and she and Sam are making preparations for the birth. I notice a small Moses basket on the sitting-room floor, along with nappies, baby talc, Sudocrem and tiny vests.

Several days pass and I am about to despair of finding a place when James phones. He tells me about a third-floor flat that's coming up for rent in the building where he lives. It's near Camden, at the bottom of Primrose Hill, and is about to be sublet by a cellist who is on contract to an American orchestra.

'It's a good place,' he says that evening when he comes round to tell me about it. 'And we'll be neighbours. Can you cope with that?' He gives me a cup of tea and hands one to Sue, who is reading the paper at the patio window, and then sits down at the kitchen table and looks at me, his brown eyes paler in the light.

My hand is under my chin and I smile across at him. 'When could I see it?' I ask.

'Think Paul's leaving in a day or two. He's a quiet bloke, keeps to himself a lot. The main living room is shaped like this . . . ' James takes the pencil from behind his ear and sits down beside me to make a sketch on a piece of newspaper. He is used to explaining himself by drawing and there are still smudges of dust on his high forehead and through his cropped hair.

'He's at the top of the house and there's this great window overlooking the park, see here.' He shades in the fuzzy heads of trees.

It sounds too good to be true.

'New Year's Eve last year, it was really frosty and he invited everyone in the house up for a drink and we opened the window and I swear there was this amazing sky burning with stars.' He sits back, placing the pencil behind his ear, and rests his right ankle casually on his left knee.

'It's probably gone already. I'm afraid to get my hopes up.' I look from Sue to James.

'James says the agent hasn't seen it yet. Might just be lucky this time.' Sue regards us both with a big smile.

'If you're on,' James says, 'I'll see Paul and set up an appointment for you. They'll need references and a note of your earnings. Might be no harm to bring that stuff along with you.'

It turns out that the agent is able to show the flat at lunchtime the following day or at six. I make arrangements to meet at the house after work. The living room looks out over a neighbouring terrace to the trees in the park. It's bright and catches the evening sun. The wooden floor has a soft sheen and the galley kitchen is old but spotless. They are looking for a caretaker agreement along with rent because there are some books and scores on the shelves and an old matrimonial brass bed that nestles in one corner, with a keyboard next to it. I ask if use of the keyboard is included in the rent and the agent asks if I play and agrees that an arrangement can be made. It is Patrick I'm thinking of.

The sight of the keyboard is a good omen, and I love the prospect of the spring bed. Already I can imagine that we will be happy here and he will come and go, with his own key. The flat has a bare lived-in feel. There's also a place to keep a car for when he stays. There and then I offer to make a deposit. Instead the agent hands me a contract and promises to ring once he has spoken to Paul.

Patrick phones from Italy. He is at a loose end spending a day at the Uffizi. Kate is with her grandmother and has already settled in.

'How are you?' I ask.

'It's been too long. I'm tired of being away.' The phone line crackles.

'You're tired of Italy?' London is a rainy day at the window.

'It's too hot and I miss you.' He has been gone for

almost a week.

'Next time I'm coming with you,' I assure him.

'I've just been to the Botticelli room. Those Madonnas are getting to me. His religious paintings are composed perfectly and the colours gorgeous, but once he changes theme the transformation is extraordinary.'

My memory of the Venus is vague. Doesn't she have red hair?

'I thought you were bored with Italy?'

'There's air conditioning in the gallery and I felt you were with me.'

'I've got one or two surprises for you.' I'm suddenly excited thinking of the flat, but decide that the news has to wait.

'A surprise?' he ponders. 'Everything all right?'

'It'll keep,' I say.

'It'll keep?' he echoes. 'What are you doing today?'

I don't tell Patrick that I've been busy putting things into boxes and that the agent has rung to arrange a meeting for a signing of the contract. There is a limit to what I can take with me to the flat and some of the books will have to go to Oxfam.

'Spring cleaning. Getting ready for Sue's baby.'

'The house is ready,' he said then. 'Kate even helped me to clear it.'

'We'll talk about that later.'

'We'll have to think about redecoration. See you Saturday?'

'Saturday.'

'I won't be late. I'll ring from the airport.'

TWENTY-EIGHT

The evening Patrick returns, Sue has already left with Sam for the maternity hospital. We go upstairs and lie down on the bed together. My head rests on his shoulder and his lips are pressed to my hair.

'Shhh . . .' he murmurs when I begin to speak about Kate, running his fingers along my hairline and temple, as if naming something by talking about it makes it worse. We both know that things have changed. There's a palpable strain in the air. The world we shared up to a couple of weeks ago is somehow over. We're both thinner. His skin has browned in the Italian sun. He caresses my spine in his familiar way.

'Is there time before we go?' he whispers. 'I'd like to.'

I've booked a table at a local Greek restaurant.

'Please?' He strokes my hair and turns to look me in the face.

It doesn't feel right. It's hard to explain. It's not to do with time.

I draw his hand from where it rests between my breasts and sit up.

'Everything's all right now,' he chides me. 'I told you. I talked to Gilly and Kate.'

I hold still next to him, surprised by my own reaction.

'I'm sorry I was away. It made the break even longer. I promise no more separations. It's over now.' He sits up straight and places an arm round my shoulder.

'How could it be?' I ask, shocked. 'Bad enough Kate, but Gilly, the police, everyone in the office. All knowing.'

'I know,' he agrees. 'But as outcomes go, it could be much worse and . . .' He leaves the sentence unfinished.

The sense of estrangement is my own. He's been too caught up in the search to find Kate.

'Can't we move on?' he asks patiently.

We start to talk about the days he spent in Italy. He goes downstairs and comes back with his leather shoulder bag and hands me a present wrapped in gold paper.

'Something from Florence.'

The packet is hard on one side and soft on the other. I'm about to pull the string to open it when he reaches a hand out to stop me.

'Don't open it now,' he says, taking the present from me and placing it on the small table beside the bed. He takes my hand in his and looks down at me. 'I'd like to undress you,' he whispers.

'Later,' I say, slipping from the bed.

We walk to the restaurant two streets away. I've been there before, with Sam, one night when Sue was resting. When we arrive, a waiter shows us to our table.

'She's still very much in favour of the idea and in better form.' Patrick is talking about Kate as he pulls back a chair and sits down. He is referring to her moving into his house. Her grandmother has enrolled her in a summer camp. 'Perhaps over the month she'll grow up a little bit,' he says, as I settle myself opposite.

'Miniskirts and motorbikes?' I suggest.

He makes a face. 'She helped me to clear a workspace for you in the house. The small room overlooking the front garden. I'll help with the move. It'll probably take two trips?' He reaches into his pocket, takes something out and places it in my hand. Keys.

'Thanks . . .' I falter. 'I've been meaning to tell you –'

'Why don't you choose for me?' he interrupts, putting away his menu.

'I know you'd prefer it if I moved in immediately, but I did some thinking while you were away, and decided it would be better all round if I found somewhere temporary.'

He doesn't say anything for a moment. It is as though I can hear a clock ticking. His silence is awesome.

'But we've been over this. We'll have a whole month before Kate moves in. The house needs repainting, thought you might like to choose colours?' He rolls up the sleeves of his denim shirt and mops the hair off his forehead, which gleams brown from the sun. That summer suits him so is not lost on me. I meet the expanding dark of his pupils.

When the waiter comes to take our order, I still haven't looked at the menu. He suggests vegetarian moussaka and we both agree.

'Come on,' Patrick urges me impatiently.

The waiter pours red wine into two glasses. Our glasses touch. It would be easy to forfeit the deposit.

'I've found a flat.'

His brow furrows and he stares at me as if he hadn't heard. 'You've what?'

'I've found something about twenty minutes west of here. It's on the third floor, lovely old feel to it. I've been offered a sublet, it's light and airy. Sue's brother James lives downstairs.'

He looks at me blankly. There's Greek music in the background and a family group at the next table, children, several adults, a grandmother. Men with curly black hair and unshaven faces, women in cotton dresses. The children are blowing bubbles into their drinks and the adults are laughing.

'Eve, you don't need to run away,' he says as if he understands for the first time my confusion. 'You're not responsible for Kate.'

The black couple by the window glance at us. The woman's hand is on the table and the man is caressing the wedding ring on her finger.

'Still. She's only a kid and we need space and privacy.' What I don't say is that I can't bear the uncertainty she causes.

'You could have told me.' His voice is calm.

'It's just for the winter. The lease expires early next year. We've not had the chance to talk lately.'

'I thought we'd agreed you're moving in. The other day when . . .' He breaks off in exasperation. 'Don't you want us to settle down?'

It would be easy to pretend there is only one world, his world. In comparison, my day-to-day life is so much less pressing. I go to work and that's important, but when I come home my life is my own. If I live on coffee and takeaways and stay out all night, the only one it troubles is myself. What's more, I like the feeling of insignificance. What I shared with Patrick I thought was ours alone until Kate went missing. In the face of her insecurity, it is hard to stand up for myself, but the words utter themselves.

'You left me out on a limb while she was gone. Something got damaged.'

What I've said puts a finger on something he is struggling to move away from.

'I had no control over it,' he says, and then adds, 'James

Corrigan is Sue's brother?' There's a hint of caution in his tone.

'That's right. We met again about three months ago, the first time since we were at school.'

'He's your age?' Patrick asks quietly. His look is hard.

'A year or two older. He was in the class ahead of me. He's fond of horses and . . .' I pause and reach for my glass and sip some red wine.

Patrick raises his eyebrows. 'And have you seen much of him?'

I haven't told Patrick about the riding lessons; there never seemed to be an ideal moment. But I know that James's friendship is too important to hide.

'We go riding sometimes, and he was a help when it came to finding the flat.'

By the time the waiter arrives with the moussaka and fills our glasses again we are sitting in silence. Neither of us wants to eat.

'We agreed that if I spoke to Kate . . .' he protests suddenly.

'I didn't expect to bring the house down.'

His urgency is claustrophobic. 'Don't tell me you put me through all this just to hang out in some flat!'

Having my own place has a glamour and security that eludes him completely. He has forgotten what it is to be twenty-six. I pick at the food on my plate.

'You've signed a contract?' He puts some food on his fork.

'I've signed a contract.' My tone is resigned.

'You could ring and cancel.' He chews and swallows some food slowly.

There's something I don't understand about the way he has come to this decision, taken our living together as given, despite recent events.

The door of the restaurant is open onto the street. All the tables are occupied. The air is still warm.

'Have you forgotten how badly you wanted this?' He arches his back and looks at me scornfully.

I think back to that time and how quickly I was drawn to him, long before I was fully aware of it.

'So?' I don't like his tone.

'Are you saying you don't want us to be family . . . you, me, Kate, and perhaps our own . . . ' His voice trails.

I smile now and appeal to him with my eyes, light-headed at the thought of pregnancy.

He doesn't respond and sits in silence, his hand under his chin.

'It's true,' I say. 'I'm not interested in settling down any more. If you love me, you'll let me find my own way with all of that.'

'You want proof of love?' he storms. 'You don't think the last month was proof enough?'

Heads start to turn around us.

'If we're meant to live together and to have a baby, it'll happen.' I'm beginning to sound like my mother. The sudden thought of her makes me wish I'd brought him to Kerry. 'We can go away together, make a trip on the boat. Or take a few days off and go to Dingle?'

Tired of the bickering, I catch the waiter's eye and call for the bill. The waiter returns and places a note on the table.

'I'm not looking for diversion.'

I take my credit card from my wallet and pay the bill.

We walk back to the house, our hands awkwardly by our sides, both disconsolate. I check the answering machine for word of Sue. There's a message from Sam to say that she's doing fine, and he'll ring again after the birth.

'If it's her first, it might take the night,' Patrick says.

'Was hoping you'd stay?' I reach out and touch his hand. The ambivalence is gone. I am aching to lie down with him and be in the same place when we wake. 'Don't you want to open the present with me?'

'Not now,' he says firmly.

'We could walk over to the flat tomorrow?'

'Maybe you'll find that solitude isn't all it's cracked up to be.'

He's tired and annoyed, and leaner than I've ever seen him in a pale jacket and denims. It's almost dark outside and the light from the stained-glass lamp casts shadows on the walls.

He is about to leave and I want to hit him.

The cool air penetrates the long blue shift I'm wearing over a T-shirt, and I rub my arms.

'Gilly's applied for a job in Brussels. I want us to stand together on this, and Kate needs to see that.'

'We can still stand together.'

He moves closer and kisses me on the forehead and puts his arms around me. His lips brush mine.

'I'm sorry,' I say finally, unsure of why I'm saying it.

He stares beyond me, then walks to the door and without a word goes into the night.

I climb the stairs, undress, slip under the covers and fall into a deep slumber. I wake from a dream in a cold sweat and realise that a hand weighs heavily on the covers when I try to move them back. For a moment I am afraid to move.

It is Patrick's arm and he is lying beside me, face down on top of the covers. His sleeping presence, offered so openly, is such an unexpected gift that the nightmarish anxiety of the dream abates. I lie quite still and ease myself closer to him and trace my fingers through the silhouette of fine hair at the back of his head and touch my lips to his forehead.

TWENTY-NINE

Still next to me when we wake, he reaches under the covers for my nakedness and he is both at his most ferocious and most gentle when we make love. Wordless and sultry afterwards, he is still getting used to the idea of me living alone. I check the answering machine and hear Sam's exhausted voice. After fourteen hours of labour, Sue has given birth to a baby boy. I relay the news to Patrick.

He stays to see the flat, and paces restlessly between the tiny kitchen and the bedroom in a way that excites me, ill at ease in such a small space, like a caged animal. This despite his particular liking for the confinement of the boat and the self-containment needed in sharing such close quarters with others. It is as if he is unsure how to fit into this new arrangement of our lives.

The young musician subletting is on contract to an American orchestra and will be back in the country in the spring. Paul is short, with longish hair and glasses. For the coming months I undertake to look after his small apartment. He needs a guarantee that I'll leave on the date agreed. Patrick hovers about, glaring at him darkly as if such an idea is an insult. Outside the house, his tone is preoccupied, but his arm is round my shoulder. He offers to drive me back to Sue's before he leaves for home but his manner is brisk and I have the feeling that he would prefer to rush away and suggest instead my taking the tube to save him a journey. He walks away in the direction of the car and I stand in the street in some confusion. He hasn't said goodbye or asked if we will meet during the week and, for a second, as people walk past me in both directions, I want to call out to him. But I turn and head for Camden station.

Back at Sue's afterwards, I finally open the present and find a book on the paintings of Botticelli. Leafing through it, I find he has marked *The Madonna and Child* with a brief note in the margin, dating his visit to the gallery and his phone call to me. As well as the book, the package contains a blue silk dress that falls like water between my fingers.

By the time Sue comes home with baby Ian, I've already packed my books into boxes, and my clothes, except for the ones I'm using, into a large suitcase. When I get back from work one evening, the baby bath is on the kitchen table and she tests the warm water by dipping her elbow into it, and the baby lies on his back on soft towels, his mouth already sucking a tiny fist. The house is a warm cocoon of slumber and baby smells, and Sue moves about in a dressing gown until midday.

'Hope he didn't wake you last night?' she enquires, as I roll up my sleeves and offer to help.

'I slept like a log,' I tell her. In fact, I'd been unable to sleep, not because of the baby, but disturbed by Patrick's continuing moodiness.

'He woke for a feed at about two and cried when I put him down, so we took it in turns to hold him. Sam got up for work at seven. He's gone upstairs for a nap now.'

She lifts the baby and places him in the water, expertly holding him on his back while she sponges water over him.

Would Patrick like to have a son, I wonder, as I watch her. What if we had a girl?

The baby's eyes dilate at the sensation and the small fists open. I stare amazed at his long fingers. She sponges water on the dark hair of his head, which stands up straight as if gelled, and the baby blinks and starts to cry. The water courses over his skin until it glistens.

'Pour some shampoo onto my palm.' Sue extends a wet hand and I squeeze a couple of drops from the bottle.

'I'll hold him for a while if you like, after the bath.'

She nods and yawns. 'Great. That way I'll get to sleep with Sam again. Forget sex. It's sleep that makes the world go round.'

The baby lies on a yellow towelling mat as Sue dries his hair and skin. She runs her finger over his scalp and shows me the delicate hollow of the fontanel. A shiver runs down my spine when I touch it.

'How can you stand it?' I ask, withdrawing my hand as Sue fastens the nappy and draws the sleeves of an ivory babygrow, covered in tiny fish, over one arm and then the other, all the while supporting his head.

'All that fragility and dependence, you mean?' she says, and just smiles.

'He's got your eyes and nose but he's got Sam's hair.'

Sue laughs and wraps the baby lightly in a soft blanket edged with satin and woven with silk ribbons, and hands him to me. 'There you go.'

I sit in the basket chair holding the baby close while Sue tidies away the bath and places baby things in a holdall and goes outside to put the towel on the line. The dark red roses are still in bloom in the garden and sunlight hangs in the air.

'We're wondering,' she calls from the garden, 'if you'd like to be godmother? James has agreed to be godfather.'

'*Like* it?' I say, 'I'd love it.' I smile at Ian, who's trying to move his fist into his mouth, and wonder what godmothers do. 'The thought of it gives me goose bumps. Do you think I'll be able?'

Sue returns through the open door.

'Now you know what it feels like to be a parent,' she answers, a fresh towel round her neck from the line. 'I'm off for a shower.'

I switch on the radio and listen to Billie Holiday singing 'I Get Along Without You Very Well'. I rock Ian gently to the music and for minutes imagine that I'm holding Patrick's baby. It's a track from *Lady in Satin* and I've heard it several times in his car. The invitation to be godmother, along with the plaintive lyrics, bring an atmosphere of calm and the baby finds his fist again, and makes little sucking noises before falling asleep. He's so still it's hard to tell if he's breathing.

It's Thursday evening and the song of a blackbird drifts in from the garden. This weekend will be my last with Sue and Sam. I'm moving out early on Sunday and the agent is going to drop the keys with Carol, who lives close by, and she's helping me to move in.

I call in to Patrick's office the next afternoon to see if he's free for a drink. He's been at a book-sellers' conference for most of the week. As I reach his door I feel nervous and anxious, and when I enter and cross the room to where he's at his desk writing, the sense of uncertainty between us increases. He remains seated, pale and cool, and leafs through some papers.

'The presents are wonderful,' I say, more loudly than I intend. It sounds like a boast.

He closes the file slowly and shrugs as if embarrassed.

'Tired of your own space already?' He begins to write again.

'I'm only moving in on Sunday. Sue's asked me to be godmother, along with James,' I blurt out.

'How very cosy.' He frowns.

'Will you come with us to the christening next week?'

'Christening?' he repeats, meeting my eyes.

'You should see the baby,' I add for something to say, unhappy at his reticence. What I really want is for us to leave the office together. There's no doubt in my mind that the sight of a sleeping infant would only do his heart good, and something in me wants to see him hold it.

'Sure,' he says vaguely, but doesn't ask about Sue, or if I need help with moving. He gets up and moves past me to the window. 'I've made other plans for this evening. Otherwise I'd come with you now,' he says, all the time looking out the window.

It is hard not to walk over and take his hand and insist that whatever arrangements he has made must wait.

'I'll give you a ring tomorrow,' he says finally.

On Sunday, once everything is in the car, Sue stands at the wrought iron gate along with Sam, who holds Ian in his arms, and we hug each other. She will visit with Ian and I'll baby-sit once they're ready to leave him for a couple of hours. Or I'll look after him while they go for a nap. Carol's car is packed to the roof and they wave us off.

Before we unpack my things, I mention Patrick's vagueness.

'He was to speak to you himself,' she says, standing in the middle of the room, boxes of books lying open on the floor.

We've run up and down the three flights of stairs a dozen times, until the Ford Fiesta is finally empty. The kettle is on and I search in a box for coffee.

'He came across to my house on Friday evening,' she says slowly.

'Oh?' I say in surprise, spooning fresh coffee from the packet into a cafetière. I'm annoyed at hearing about Patrick yet again from Carol.

'That time Kate was gone, we became quite close. He was very distressed and both Gilly and the police were giving him a hard time.'

'Yeah. I know. You're up there with the saints.'

The kettle switches itself off and I pour boiling water into the glass jug and set the plunger on top.

'You don't need to be sarcastic.' Carol takes off her glasses and rubs her eyelids.

'The cops were trawling the country for Kate, and Patrick was doing his nut. You were Florence Nightingale.' I set glazed mugs on the tray, two from the set I brought from Dingle, along with a matching jug and bowl for milk and sugar.

'He was upset that you signed a contract for the flat without consulting him.'

'I know. You like being the one to pick up the pieces?' I pour the coffee and hand her one.

'Perhaps I do.' She tastes the coffee. 'Thanks. That should hit the spot.'

'Don't feel bad about that.' I'm still angry with Patrick.

She sighs deeply. After a long silence she begins to speak again. 'Anyway, I reminded him that while Kate was missing, he was difficult to reach.' She smiles. 'I did say that it would probably be easier all round, now that you have your own place.'

'Thanks,' I say. 'You're a pal.'

'We go back a long way,' she explains and smiles a winsome, seductive smile and I see in her something I've overlooked before. The sympathetic and reliable friend could be an extremely attractive rival. It struck me that she and Patrick were likely companions. Had it not occurred to either of them before now?

'That's not all I have to tell you,' she adds enigmatically. 'I never expected things to move so quickly . . .'

'Oh?' I say abruptly.

'Pete was there as well on Friday night. You know we met recently, and I promised to cook dinner. So we celebrated my fortieth and Kate's return with Patrick.'

'How is Pete?' I ask, looking around and thinking that it would be fun to organise a party for Carol in my new flat.

She says nothing for several seconds but looks keenly at my face. 'He's very well. It's so much better the second time round,' she adds.

'So what happened?'

'After Patrick left, we had another bottle and got a bit tipsy. We were just saying goodnight, and I could see that he didn't want to leave . . .'

'But you had other ideas?'

Carol is innately cautious. She looks bashful and struggles with memory. 'We just stood there listening to the silence of the night with our arms round each other and . . . we kissed and I asked him if he'd like to stay.'

She blushes and takes off her glasses, calmly lays them on the table and looks at me as if she's showing me her beautiful oval eyes for the first time.

'Was it a mistake?' she asks, as if there was a scientifically correct answer to such a question.

'How do you feel about it?'

Up to now I was oblivious of the small signs of infatuation in her looks and dress. She is wearing a different scent and her hair, gathered in a roll at the back of her head, falls in loose wisps round her face. Her expression is altogether clearer and brighter.

'Who knows where it will lead?' she adds dreamily.

'Who knows?' I smile. 'That's exactly how I feel too.

There's been so many ups and downs with Patrick and he's very moody of late. I have the house keys. I'll maybe go across later and see him.'

We stand in silence opposite the window. She looks around the flat to admire the morning's work. It still looks empty.

'I hope you'll be happy here.'

She scans the trees below the window. We watch the couples strolling in the park.

The overcast sky to the north and west opens out above the terraces on the far side. The view from the window brings to mind the fuchsia hedges that run in front of my mother's house and the tiny patch of ocean that can be seen from an upstairs window. We could tell if the tide was low or high by listening for the din of waves on the shore. Even if the tide was full and barely moving, it was possible to hear a wave break over rocks further out. At this height, wind in the trees sounds like the sea running through pebbles.

Summer is nearly over.

'You must come to Essex one weekend to meet my parents,' she says, picking up the tray and taking it to the worktop in the kitchen.

'Sometime in September? My mother is visiting last week of August.'

'Of course,' she replies. 'I'd like to meet her.' She is about to take her leave.

'I want to show her London.' I turn to look out the window again.

'See you in the office?' she calls from the hallway, before carefully making her descent on the stairs.

THIRTY

After Carol goes, I lie face down for a long time on a patchwork quilt with appliqué designs, a house, a boat, an anchor, a tree, a man, a woman, a child, in each square. The colours are burgundy and indigo, on a white cotton background. It is old and was made by a grandaunt who lived in Chicago. 'If I come to London, I want to be warm,' my mother had said, putting it in my suitcase. Now I know that my own flat is the right decision. Since James befriended me, the world has become a calmer, more reliable place.

I close my eyes. It has been no length of time since I was on the Heath with Patrick, lying beneath a tree. The last time we went there, he'd sat with his back to the trunk, and I lay on the grass before him, watching the sun through the leaves cast a dappled fretwork on the grass.

'What are you thinking?' I'd asked, held by the animated stillness of his body.

'Wherever thou goest, I will go with thee,' he'd said softly, lifting my bare heel and rubbing the sole of my foot with his warm hands. The underarm of his shirt was damp with perspiration and he'd unbuttoned his shirt, exposing the soft flesh of his chest. The heat had been soporific.

I decide to go unannounced to his house. Seeing him might reduce the uncertainty of abandonment and staying away would only prolong the agony. Taking back the keys gives me a pretext to go over that afternoon.

When I arrive at his house and ring the bell, it is after five and piano music drifts from the room at the back. Through the window I see that the patio door is open and conclude that Patrick must be in the garden. I put the key in the lock and open the door, and walk into the sitting room, where Bach's *Goldberg Variations* are playing quietly on the CD player.

Patrick is sitting on a garden chair, facing away from the house, an open book in his hand. He is wearing an old sweatshirt and denims and looks dejected and tired. I want to reach out to touch and soothe him, but I just stand there watching him.

The apple tree is laden with fruit, not yet fully ripened. Some roses growing across the hedge from a neighbour's garden spill their petals onto grass beside the tree. The scent of barbecue smoke is in the air and there is the sound of a party a few gardens away.

It would be easy to let him know I'm there and for a moment I am overwhelmed by the thought of just walking over and sitting close to him. My eyes are focused on the skin of his hand resting on his lap. For now, he has chosen not to make contact. I tiptoe silently backwards into the hall.

My feet carry me swiftly along the pavement and it feels as if I dare not breathe. My heart is pounding and everything in sight is vivid and clear: faces of people I pass on the street, their eyes meeting or avoiding mine; the rustle of scraps of paper along the curb that leads to the station; the shape of a building seen in isolation from its surroundings.

Before I know it, I'm slipping my weekly travel card through the ticket stile and standing on the platform. The automatic time schedule lists the next train in seven minutes. It's five twenty and less than half an hour since I walked off the train on the opposite side.

Across from me, a young black man and a small boy, both dressed in baseball caps, T-shirts and blue jeans, sit together in the weather shelter. The boy has his hand about his father's neck and gazes at me. I look and turn away and he starts to play peekaboo. He shrieks his delight when I catch him out. The pleasure is in being found, rather than in hiding. As the train draws in, the man takes the boy's hand and smiles at me. I resolve to talk to Patrick as soon as possible.

As I walk along the railings at the bottom of Primrose Hill it is sunny and warm, and the blue sky is broken with cumulus clouds that trail in masses from the direction of the river, like mounds of white bed linen. I hear the din from the children's playground in the park, and a light breeze blows in my face.

It is too warm to go inside and I decide instead to browse in small shops that are still open along Chalk Farm. The sun is shining on one side of the street and I pause at a window here, a flower shop there, and finally stop at a café with tables on the pavement. From the menu, I choose an iced coffee and while I wait, I close my eyes to feel the sun on my face. The sound of footsteps and of people chatting fills the quiet street. The coffee arrives, rich and cold.

On my return to the house, I meet the elderly woman who lives on the ground floor below James. Mrs Goldstein is grey-haired and she is sweeping the hallway outside her door, neatly dressed and compact in slacks and flat shoes. We say hello. She looks at me curiously. I am not altogether welcome. My age tells her that I am a potential source of loud music and conversation in the middle of the night and my nationality does nothing whatsoever to dispel that impression. Thus far I am an unknown quantity. She is sorry that Paul has gone away and asks if I also play the cello. She tells me which day the rubbish is collected and where to find the nearest grocery and bottle bank.

That first night on my own, moonlight falls through the skylight window. I have left the blind open and a solitary star in darkness holds my attention. Once as a student when I lost blood from an accident and passed out dizzy, I woke in hospital to find my mother's freckled hand resting on the starched sheet next to me. I stared at the hand and then at Melanie gazing at me, her presence as inimical to that etherised atmosphere as a summer meadow. Her first time in Dublin! How did she come to be there and so quickly?

I lie watching the night sky. Would I ever tell her about Patrick, his ability to walk away? For the first time I begin to understand how she felt when my father walked away from her. I cannot sleep. The birds start to wake and the sky is changing to a lightless metal. Soon it will be day and there's work to face and, somehow, Patrick.

THIRTY-ONE

The next day, leaving the office, we run into each other at the side door just after five thirty. He turns to wait for me.

'Look who's here!' he comments. 'Let me see you. Your cheeks are pale.' He falls into step beside me and we go through the back gate.

'Walk me to the train?' I suggest, because he is at a loss for words.

'Primrose Hill?' He reads the tension on my face.

We walk along the street under the heavy leafiness of trees towards the railings of the park, our eyes not daring to meet. The air is cool and blustery, the colours of the leaves changing.

'I'm sorry I've been so removed.' His voice is quieter, more confidential.

'Not from what Carol has told me.' I would like to let him know that I'd been to his house. Instead I search for his keys in my pocket and feel them in my hand.

'Carol?' he asks vaguely.

His evasiveness annoys me. 'You spent an evening with her?'

'So I did. Pete Murray was there too. Hadn't seen him for years.' He shrugs complacently and places his hands in his pockets as he strolls along. He is calm and unconcerned. 'We had a couple of drinks. Celebrated her fortieth, far as I know they're together again. Pete was staying the night. I was going to call over on Sunday, in fact, and left a message at your old number, but wasn't sure exactly when you were moving.'

'I told you I was moving on Sunday.' My tone is resigned.

'Give me some credit for letting you get on with things,' he complains.

I take the keys from my pocket. 'I should give you back these. Shouldn't I?' I add softly, 'At least for now.'

He takes them from my hand. 'What are you telling me?'

'That it hasn't been easy in the last few months and you walked away from me again the other day and I didn't know what was going on.' As I speak, my anger rises, and tears spring to my eyes. 'In fact, I called to your house yesterday.'

'Why didn't you come inside and have a drink?' His tone is casual.

'I let myself in and you were sitting in the garden reading. I wanted to speak to you, to tell you that there was no need to punish me again.' We are almost at the brow of the hill. Tears are running down my face and he takes out a handkerchief and hands it to me and I dry my eyes.

'I came to the conclusion that there was something going on between you and James,' he says slowly and looks me in the eye for the first time.

We are at the top of the hill, and I stand still for a moment. Even though my cheeks are red, the breeze is cool on my face.

'Come on, Eve. First he manages to wake up in the same house as you every morning. And now you're to be godparents. And you go horse-riding together.'

I realise that Patrick has already concluded that James is more than a friend. It's not something I can deny.

'Since I met him, I feel more at home in London,' I admit hesitantly, hearing again the clamour of hoofs behind me and seeing James stand on the stirrups as he galloped along, his whole body tuned to the speed, his face transported.

We move downhill together to where the light is breathtaking.

'How's Kate?' I ask.

He sweeps the hair from his forehead. 'Happy.'

'It's for the best then.'

'She's getting her books for school and she's excited about letting her friends know of *the big move*,' he says, with a hint of regret.

'I was too wilful.'

'Talk about intransigence.'

'We Irish have lots of practice. About six hundred years.'

It will soon be September. The light is almost yellow, the year turning. We make the final descent quickly. I watch sunlight coming off grass in brilliant green.

'I'd like to see your flat now, with your pictures on the wall and your books on the shelf.' He is hesitant and when I don't answer immediately he adds, 'I'd like to walk you home.'

'I need to think about it. Perhaps another time?'

We are approaching the gate of the park and our steps slow to a stop and he moves a strand of hair from my face.

We are interrupted by the voices of a group of Japanese tourists crowding round the notice board behind us at the gate.

A young man with a rather pointed face turns to ask me to

take a photograph and hands over the camera. I might be sleepwalking. Individuals place themselves in three rows of an extended family, grandparents, couples, teenagers. It is a struggle to focus the lens and my hand is shaking.

Afterwards I join Patrick and we continue through the gate.

'That reminds me. There are some photos I want to show you and I came across some things of yours in the house. Your red scarf, a black T-shirt. Your fur trim jacket . . .' He pauses. 'So you were there with me in a way the week Kate went missing. Every time I came across them they were a comfort, as if they were holding your spirit.'

'It's kind of you to say that. Perhaps in a week or two we might meet for lunch?' I smile. 'This time next week my mother will be here.'

'Of course, I'd forgotten.' His tone is distanced. 'That reminds me, how is Sue getting along?'

'She's great. Sam got us tickets for the Nina Simone concert at Ronnie Scott's. She's going to take the baby for a while.'

Then we walk on along the busy pavement, not speaking because we have to walk at a pace. Once we reach the street where I live, I stop walking and turn to him.

'This is it,' I say.

'This is as far as it goes?' He leans down and places a kiss on my forehead. At the sudden contact, it is all I can do to turn on my heels and walk towards the steps of my house that lead to the white wooden door.

ACKNOWLEDGEMENTS

Hans Massaquoi has noted that it usually takes a village of loyal relatives, friends and professionals to raise a book, and that it's not unlike raising a child. *One Room an Everywhere* is no exception.

To colleagues and friends who read the story my gratitude for their generosity of spirit and advice: Renate Ahrens, Siobhán Parkinson, John Hobbs, Niall MacMonagle, Mary Rose Binchy, Sue Fahy, Trish Yarrow, and Louise Dobbin.

I give credit and thanks to colleagues that I met many years ago on my journey of becoming a writer who are a steady source of wisdom and humour: Sheila Barrett, Alison Dye, Cecelia McGovern, Joan O'Neill, and Julie Parsons.

My appreciation to Niamh Morris for reading the first draft and promptly finding me an agent, and to Faith O'Grady of The Lisa Richards Agency for her encouragement and confidence in the work from the beginning and for negotiating with the publisher.

I would like to thank Peter Sirr and Bernadette Larkin at the Irish Writers Centre for offering work over many years; Declan Kiberd for inviting me to work as poet-in-residence at the Department of Anglo Irish Literature, University College Dublin, in Spring 2002, while Blackstaff were reading the manuscript; Keith Gibbons for technical assistance with the computer.

I cannot write this page without mentioning Blackstaff Press and especially Anne Tannahill and Patsy Horton who accepted my first novel in May 2002. For her patience and infinite care with the manuscript, my admiration and affection to freelance editor, Hilary Bell.

I am grateful to my mother and all my family and friends for their support and to Fran Gleeson for proofreading the galleys. I would like to pay tribute to my father who died in 1986 for his vision and lifelong encouragement.

Credit for encouraging this novel from conception to delivery goes to Justin, my husband. For his love, and that of my children who kept me company during the adventure of writing this story, and for their patience and prompt advice, my deep gratitude.